UP UP UP

UP UP UP

JULIE BOOKER

ANANSI

This edition published in 2011 by
House of Anansi Press Inc.
110 Spadina Avenue, Suite 801
Toronto, ON, M5V 2K4
Tel. 416-363-4343
Fax 416-363-1017
www.anansi.ca

Distributed in Canada by
HarperCollins Canada Ltd.
1995 Markham Road
Scarborough, ON, M1B 5M8
Toll free tel. 1-800-387-0117

15 14 13 12 11   1 2 3 4 5

Library and Archives Canada Cataloguing in Publication

Booker, Julie
Up, up, up / Julie Booker.

ISBN 978-0-88784-300-6

I. Title.

PS8603.O653U6   2011   C813'.6   C2010-906479-8

Jacket design: Alysia Shewchuk
Text design and typesetting: Alysia Shewchuk

 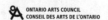

*We acknowledge for their financial support of our publishing program
the Canada Council for the Arts, the Ontario Arts Council, and the
Government of Canada through the Canada Book Fund.*

Printed and bound in Canada

For Jean Booker
first reader, best editor

GEOLOGY IN MOTION

Lorrie and Katie tended to say too much.

Imagine two fat ladies in a kayak!

In skin-tight wetsuits. Eek!

Talked up Alaska until they couldn't back out.

Over egg-white omelettes in Lorrie's kitchen, Katie read: "If you meet a bear, stretch your arms overhead and say, 'Hey, bear, hey.' The bear will come towards you, but it's a bluff charge. Only drop when he's one foot in front of you."

"What about the camper in the news last week?" Lorrie asked. "The one who got mauled."

"The grizzly was ten feet away. He dropped too soon."

"He dropped too soon," Lorrie repeated, as if measuring how close she could come to fear. Animals, she trusted. She had other things to worry about. Since the bariatric surgery she'd dropped 140 pounds. *Another 60 to go.* Katie had chosen the slow route — melba toast and tuna — but the scales held stubborn at 280.

Lorrie didn't know why a flashlight was on the gear list from the kayak company, considering the twenty-four hours of daylight. She and Katie went shopping for neoprene gloves, inflatable Therm-a-Rests, checking the strength of the nozzles. Oversize Gore-Tex pants were difficult to find. In Mountain Equipment Co-op Lorrie and Katie lay on the floor in XL sub-zero sleeping bags, trying to imagine the frigid night air. Drawstrings tight under their noses. The manager smirked, made them practise stuffing themselves into the sleep sacks like two giant blue pills.

‹ ‹ ‹

At the Anchorage airport Lorrie said a quiet prayer of thanks that they were going to Seward. They weren't joining the lineup of men boarding a small craft to go farther into the bush. Their overgrown beards and never-cut hair, second-skin parkas and dusty knapsacks. Two dour Native women in line with the bushmen. As if the loudspeaker had called, "Last flight to Severe Depression."

It took a while to get to Miss Cathy's B & B. As the van passed through town, Lorrie watched the back of Katie's little-girl head peer out the window. *When did she go grey?* Her hair in a tight ponytail on top like a fountain, ends spilling down towards her triple chin. Not that Lorrie felt superior. Before the surgery she too had worn her hair high, like a bird's nest. Anything to draw the eye up.

"The Yukon Bar Steakhouse. Hobo Jim's Pizza. Sourdough Bakery." Katie whispered the names as if they themselves might bring on the weight. "Everything's poison to me but no reason you can't live a little now that you're nice and slim. And look, Chinese right here in Alaska."

The B & B had a rusted iron bed frame at the end of the driveway, flowers growing through the springs. Miss Cathy waved as she crossed the yard, her figure trim, not counting the beer belly.

"How are you girls?" Her voice raw from cigarettes. "You're in the Bear's Den, around the back. How long you staying?"

"Just tonight. We're off to Northwestern Lagoon tomorrow."

Miss Cathy's mouth dropped. "You girls got balls."

She unlocked the cabin door, handed them the bear-paw keychain. "Don't be lookin' so worried. That ain't real bear. It's squirrel. The kitchen's in the back of the house. Help yourself to whatever."

"Jeezus," Lorrie said, once Miss Cathy was gone.

The room barely held the two of them turning sideways, *Pardon me.* They shimmied around the bed. Katie fell back, smothering a dozen black bears in migration across the comforter. Lorrie held up two cushions in front of her breasts, shook them so the tassels quivered.

"Are those teeth?" Katie said.

Lorrie inspected the tassels. "Plastic."

Katie turned to the side table, tapped the nodding heads of three miniature grizzlies.

They wandered through the backyard, the tangle of wildflowers. The outhouse door was open, a flush toilet ·

inside. They went in the back door, past stalagmite magazine piles, knives and forks on a laundry machine like weeds in cups, into the kitchen, where Lorrie made herself some green tea beneath the sign LIFE IS SHORT. EAT DESSERT FIRST.

Katie filled a bowl with Honeycomb, brought the box with her from the kitchen.

The two of them sat at a round dining table that cut into their bellies, looking at the framed maps, sailor figurines, and dusty nautical instruments. Books crowded the shelves. A ship's porthole leaned back on the sideboard, its glass filthy, a murky Jesus behind. His arms open, pointing to the surrounding titles: *Finding Health. Healing Yourself.*

"That new appetite suppressant's making me hungrier," Katie said between mouthfuls. "And the nightmares. I drop off for an hour and wake up thinking, *Now where did that come from?*"

With Katie smack up against her in the bed, Lorrie tried to sleep, but the midnight sun called to her through the drawn curtains. She went for a walk along the highway. *Surgery won't help a bit if you don't change the way you live.* Cars whizzed by her. All this way for pine trees and asphalt. When she returned to the Bear's Den, she found Katie asleep on her back. One arm high across her stomach, anchoring herself, the other hanging over the side of the bed, her fingers twitching in the icy Pacific, dangling from the edge of a kayak. A nightmare probably taking hold right then.

‹ ‹ ‹

"Most visitors do a half-day jaunt in Resurrection Bay. Some go farther out, to Aialik Bay," Wendy, their guide, explained the night before the excursion. When they'd showed up at Alaska's Here, Wendy was kind enough not to do the usual full-body scan of Lorrie and Katie, not to scowl at the obvious challenges. "Our water taxi will take your gear and kayaks out to the farthest bay west of Seward." Wendy was rosy-faced, fresh out of college. The type that burns energy just standing still.

"Northwestern, where the glaciers calve all night like thunder," Wendy had said on the phone to Lorrie. "It's magical." When Lorrie had called other outfitters, they'd described their trips as nice, great, beautiful. But not magical. One thousand dollars for three days, booked solely on the hint of transformation.

On the way out to the campsite, Katie shivered in the water taxi's cabin. Lorrie stood on the deck, hanging on to the yellow recreational kayak, its cockpit larger than a sea kayak's. She'd learned the difference after a bit of a mix-up on the phone. "No, not for larger bodies of water, for *larger bodies*." Lorrie faced the wind, loving the spray on her face. She saw islands of rock, then almost-camouflaged spindle-shaped harbour seals, unabashedly sunning their big bellies. Puffins flying so low to the water she could see one's red and black eye looking at her, a dozen fish held crosswise in its beak. *Look at all the snacks.* She missed the comforts of home for a brief moment before spotting the grey bumps in the water. Porpoises. The boat gained on them. Lorrie watched their sleek bodies slipping over and through the waves, perfectly designed for play.

Farther out, Lorrie pointed at a shot of spray just ahead. She looked back at the cabin, but Katie was chatting with Wendy. Lorrie watched the whale move alongside like a shadow. It was mammoth, appropriately insulated, swimming effortlessly. She knew she was the only one who'd seen it.

The taxi dropped them on a remote stony beach. They struggled with their kayak and equipment while Wendy showed them how to pull the boats high up past the tide line. Lorrie extended the tent poles as far as she could until her arms shook and Katie took over. They draped the tent, bending without grace to pin the corners, then straightened up to get their breath back. They hammered pegs into shifting rocks, taking frequent breaks. Careful not to trample the beach greens that had survived the elements, taken hold without soil. No-trace camping meant no fires. No digging toilets. They teetered to pee at the shoreline, balanced just long enough to shit into silver foil WAG Bags.

The sun slipped behind the glacier, but it was only a dimming, a signal for the bugs to swarm. Wendy cooked while they strolled along the beach in D. H. Lawrence–style mosquito-net hats.

"I'm starving." Katie said.

"Me too."

Every time the glacier across from them thundered, they froze like space creatures stepping over moonstones. Looked up to see what had fallen. Of course they missed it every time. The sound delay about thirteen seconds.

"There. Where the new waterfall is. Where the ice is still tumbling. See it?" Lorrie said.

They sat on the rocks, lifting the nets of their hats for each swift spoonful of curried noodles. Lorrie ate watching the glacier as if it were a TV, listening to the constant sound of running water from the ice mass. When she looked over,

Wendy was ladling more soup into Katie's empty bowl. Lorrie's was still half full. *How did that happen?*

Wendy read to them before bedtime about "geology in motion." She pointed to maps printed earlier in the year that showed the glacier sitting where they now camped.

"No one's sure why the earth is warmer. It could be because we've damaged the atmosphere. But maybe our orbit's altered. Or continents are shifting near the poles, or maybe the sun itself has changed." She didn't sound sad, as if time needed to be slowed down or humans were at fault. The glaciers simply had their own journey. And while they were shrinking, heading for the sea, other geological features were expanding, like the mountains in Resurrection Bay. Tectonic plates were continually shifting. No one was to blame.

They went to sleep with the glacier framed in the tent's vestibule window. Fully lit by the night sun. Lorrie slept in shorts she would never wear in public, her sleeping bag unzipped, not needing as many layers as she'd anticipated. Ice rumbled, masses fell while Katie snored. In the morning, Lorrie pointed out to Katie where new rock face had come to the surface.

‹ ‹ ‹

The first day was a leisurely paddle following the shoreline. Katie and Lorrie shared a double kayak floating dangerously low in the water. Wendy paddled close by, sipping coffee from a Thermos. Lorrie could hear Katie, behind her, continually reaching into the Smarties trail mix Baggie on her spray deck.

They passed hanging valleys carved out by glaciers,

mountaintops rounded by migrating icebergs. There were the beginnings of moss, wildflowers — yellow, white, and pink — a lonely spruce tree springing out of grey rock. Succession forests, Wendy called them. As if they had come to the end of the earth to see the beginning.

On day two Wendy pointed in the direction of Northwestern Glacier. "That's where we're going today. Four hours' paddling."

They passed Anchor Glacier and Ogive, both topped with blue, the only colour of the spectrum able to escape the dense crystal. Ogive tiered with striations of grey rock like a fallen soufflé.

Northwestern Lagoon was a bowl surrounded by mountainous glaciers. Lorrie felt the temperature drop suddenly. Their tiny kayaks like red and yellow tinder on silt green water. The regular sound of thunder like a storm moving in. Every time Lorrie heard it she paddled faster, wanting to get there. To the source.

"This is close enough," Lorrie heard from the back of the kayak. Had Katie said it to herself or to her?

Lorrie kept paddling. Ice chunks all around, a floating sculpture garden. A flock of misshapen forms heading somewhere, in no apparent rush.

"Wendy, can you tell us where to paddle so we don't hit these?" Katie called out.

"Look, that one looks like a cormorant," Lorrie said. They banged into one, a half trout, complete in its reflection.

"Can you just tell me where to steer? I can't see what's up ahead."

"It doesn't matter if we hit the small ones, Katie." Lorrie kept paddling forward.

"Wendy," Katie called out.

"Just follow my path," Wendy said.

"Why go closer? They won't look any different."

They hit another piece of ice. Lorrie shifted a little so she could pick up the chunk and put it on the spray skirt. She'd heard that the Japanese imported it for drinks. She sucked the pointy end. The instant freezing of her lips, wet pouring down her chin, taking her back to the ice-cube diet, but this was too solid to bite into.

"I'm really not enjoying this." Katie's paddle cuffed the hull. "Just drop me off on a beach somewhere with my lunch. Pick me up on the way back."

Don't be absurd, Lorrie wanted to say. "A beach some-where" was at least three hours away. Wendy was ahead of them. The boat teetered with each erratic knock of Katie's paddle against fibreglass, but Lorrie didn't turn around. She listened to what she thought were sighs, then realized they were quick breaths. Katie stopped paddling and Lorrie sud-denly felt the weight in the rear of the kayak, and her own heaviness, how vulnerably low they sat in the water.

"Can't you tolerate it a little longer?" Lorrie said. Her paddle gentle in the water. A few more strokes; she knew that was all she had. Wendy kayaked back to them.

"You gals okay with this?"

"No," said Katie.

Lorrie longed to axe the boat in two and paddle away.

They sat watching the glaciers calve for an hour. Chunks the size of apartment buildings fell. They were so far away the waves didn't even reach them. As close as they would ever be. When the sound hit seconds later, Lorrie cheered. Wendy clapped.

"What's the big deal?" Katie said quietly.

On the way back, the floating ice chunks seemed to have multiplied. The sculptures spun from their own weight, forward and back, like gymnasts in warm-up. Crackling like bubble wrap. Wendy stayed close. Lorrie tried her best to call out, "Left," or "Big one on the right."

Wendy pointed to otters diving for their dinner. "Not an ounce of fat," she said. "A high metabolism and insulated under-fur keep them warm." The mammals floated in the sun, snacked on fish tucked under their stubby limbs, then placed their paws together as if in prayer.

Katie began to match Lorrie's rhythm as they cut into clearer water, back towards the campsite. Past Ogive and Anchor glaciers, old faces that had softened in the late daylight.

While Wendy cooked dinner, Katie and Lorrie donned their mosquito hats, perched on campstools, exhausted. Katie explained that it had all seemed too big. The height of the glaciers, the sound of thunder, the depth of the fjord, the frigid water. The space in the kayak had gotten tighter. "I almost had a full-blown panic attack. I just focused on things in front of me: the water bottle, my camera, the paddle."

"You did great." Lorrie quietly searched the beach, hoping to bring back a piece of Alaska. She had a new sense of calm. The afternoon's chaos had rippled from kayak to ocean to glacier, right down to the tectonic plates, seesawing both her and Katie onto land. Onto shifting stones that now felt solid. She held up a big rock to show Katie. A ball of granite, with streaks red, white, and grey. A perfect sample.

"Do you think I can get this through Customs?" She laughed.

"I think I'd prefer smoked salmon or chocolate bear scat from the duty-free," Katie said.

‹ ‹ ‹

They sat on the grass by the kayak shop waiting for the airport van. Katie ate the last of Lorrie's trail mix, the Smarties long gone. Lorrie looked out at Resurrection Bay. Her pants definitely felt looser. The place where the waistband usually cut a fold in her belly had shifted. A group of children spilled into the daycare yard next to them. Two supervisors organized a game of Frisbee. Some kids played patty cake under the trees, dug in the dirt, manoeuvred tiny trucks on the grass. Two boys with freshly cut hair took turns concealing a neon orange soccer ball somewhere in the yard. Under a bench, behind the garbage can, by the tree. As one walked close to it, the other called, "Warm, warmer, warmer, hot!"

Lorrie closed her eyes too while one hid the ball before calling, "Okay!" She opened her eyes. Unlike the boy, she saw it immediately. Like an Alaskan sun pulsing in the short grass. The persistent sun Lorrie missed already. Slipping behind the glacier right now without them.

When the kids ran out of hiding places, they tucked the ball into the same spots again, pretending not to notice it right away. Then they pointed to the long grass near the kayak trailer, even though the supervisor had told them not to go off the property.

The boys walked closer, exploring, then stopped when

they saw Lorrie and Katie.

"You're fat." The boy was looking at Katie but he could have been talking to Lorrie. His own layer of baby fat could go either way.

Katie stood up, in full bluff charge. It took her a few strides. She snatched the ball and called out, "Hot, burning hot!" She held it against her belly for what Lorrie felt was an excruciatingly long time. Lorrie saw the boys' faces recoil, the strength in their cheeks and jaws recede. She watched them get younger. And she knew that if Katie held on much longer, they would crack. Babies in one thundering cry.

Katie cast the ball onto the tarmac and the boys chased after it.

No matter how old we get, Lorrie thought. *No matter where we go.*

EVERY GOOD BOY

He was the shoe man at Eaton's. "Let's go see if Mr. Acker's working today," Mom would say. And we'd move among the round tables, shoes poised in cream-cake fashion on Plexiglas stands. Till we found the brown of his head bent over a lady's leg, his knees out, frog-style. Proposing marriage with a steel foot-ruler. Place arch here, a jiggling of the knob, and it was consummated. "Size eight narrow," he'd say in that London accent. Suddenly sharp-pencil tall, the pinstripe grey of his suit jacket turned so there was just a hint of shimmer. He looked me in the eye and I knew life was as serious as Buster Brown, specially made for my wide feet.

Compassionate Mr. Acker. He'd point to the orthopedic sticker inside the heel, the little blond Buster with his arm slung around his trusty dog, winking at me. *No one will know you're not average.* I loved Mr. Acker for that. And for never acting like our drop-in visits were taking him from his life's work. Even with a lineup of skirts, each lady dangling a shoe like an unlit cigarette, saying hello was as important as a size six pump, a size nine in black.

I should have known there's no such thing as a perfect man. A perfect childhood.

Mrs. Acker was my piano teacher. We'd drive out to Scarborough in the blue Chevy, my sister and I in the back seat, perched on red simulated leather. Mom swearing at each left turn, as if being in the middle of an intersection invited life to hit us full on. And when the car sputtered it was, "Goddammit, your father said he checked the car."

Dad with the dirty hanging overalls. A van full of brushes and rollers, cans dripping like candles, the latex-stained fingernails he'd scrub each night with stinky green soap. I never saw him in a suit. His shoes, spattered work boots taken off to reveal toes like fists. The book of receipts and bills left for Mom to work out on the adding machine each night. The click of red and yellow buttons as she pulled that steel arm down, punching green and red numbers onto long paper curls. Dad snoring sitting up on the couch, mouth open, catching a different dream.

The Acker life, I thought. To come home, shoes still intact. To a pixie waif, barefoot, Mia Farrow haircut, flowers dancing across her sundress, all flushed and full of music at the door. She'd have forgotten to start dinner but Beethoven and Chopin were there, her bare arms and legs. "Every Good Boy Deserves Fudge," she'd sing to him and he'd throw his arms around her belted waist and let her suck in all that shoe-polish perfume.

There appeared to be no catastrophes in the split-level bungalow on Sherwood Court. I went twice a week to prepare for my Conservatory exams. With Mrs. Acker perched on the edge of the bench, her right foot a metronome, the exhale of her cigarette between andante and allegretto, I could go right to Massey Hall. And Mr. Acker as my dad. Yes to a clear, straight-ahead life, I said.

Elspeth was the glitch. The squirt of a daughter who got her fine hair trimmed at the barber, who tortured me in her basement while I waited for my sister to complete her lesson. She rarely turned on the lamp. Games were played by the light from the upstairs hallway. Games designed and orchestrated by Elspeth. Blankets and chairs became hide-and-seek houses. Wagons became ambulances, transporting Elspeth and her dolls to hospital. Tag was played with a ball, Elspeth in the coveted role of It, taking aim at me. The room one big toy store after an earthquake. Games that fit into fifty-minute time slots, ending with Mrs. Acker's outline on the landing.

"Okay, love, your turn." My turn to be daughter. Elspeth's parents should have been mine. Our mothers must have lain side by side in the hospital in their frilly housecoats. I must have been switched at birth.

Elspeth had these blond straight-across bangs that only pointed out her lack of eyebrows and lashes. As if they'd been singed off by a firecracker and were smart enough not to grow back. Her eyes were mostly like mailbox slits until she got an idea, and then she opened them wide so you could see the rules starting.

"Let's play Blind. You go first. Wear this scarf over your eyes. I'll set up an obstacle course and then you have to trust me to guide you through. No peeking."

I listened to Elspeth rearrange things in the basement the way you listen to a dentist preparing the drill and needle and nasty bits behind you. I followed her voice, a bat's radar, stumbling and bruising my shins. I heard her giggling, "I've wet my pants!" When it was her turn to be blind, she suddenly tired of the game, went on to something else. Like Find the Treasure. One whole wall was a pile of shoeboxes. Mostly with lids. Each week she'd hide something from her mom's bedroom and we'd play Battleship in the grid of boxes.

D across, 5 down, a black penis we could twist and bend with our fingers.

G7, what I thought was a dog puppet head on a slingshot, but Elspeth said she had seen her dad wear it *down there* once.

H4, pills for her mom's head.

E3, a fish lure Elspeth called an I-U-D.

B2, an Indian sex-position book.

One time I found a card on the floor that said: *I know you've been frustrated. I'll be ready soon. You're a saint for waiting. I'm sorry. XOXX Brenda.*

"Give me that," Elspeth said, like I'd sunk her battleship.

Brenda was not a Mrs. Acker first name. It should have been Tutti or Glissando or Fairy Godmother. As if she could grant me wishes. I would have asked for that timer on the piano to disappear so my lesson could accidentally slide into early evening, with Elspeth locked in the basement. Maybe, just maybe, I would witness the homecoming of Mr. Acker. I never saw Elspeth with her dad. I was spared that image.

And Elspeth's interactions with Mrs. Acker were between lessons, a brief hug or "Why don't you girls play Sorry or Trouble if you're bored down there?"

Mom started dropping us at their sidewalk, waving from the car. One time the front door was open. "Mrs. Acker? Hello, Mrs. Acker?" She was dancing in the living room. I'd seen white bras and underwear in the Sears catalogue, full of invisible breasts and bellies, cut-outs for my paper dolls. But Mrs. Acker's panties hung on her hipbones, her bra stood away from her chest, and I could see her ribs sticking out more than anything. Her eyes were half open, her mouth twisting the same as when I missed a sharp. She was listening to something, a rhythm unlike Beethoven or Bach, her knees bending, then locking, toes making swirls in the shag carpet, arms up as if she were picking apples.

We stood there for a while, too afraid to say her name again. Then Elspeth came crashing down the stairs, saying to us, *Look, extra-long bootlaces, piles of them. We can tie each other up.* She stopped at the sight of her mother. Mrs. Acker skipped off to her bedroom, her panty bottoms sagging.

The last day of my lessons, I could hear my sister plonking away upstairs, hitting the B instead of B flat in the same place every time.

Elspeth had just opened one of the shoeboxes. *See, I did hide something after all. You never would have found it.* Two orange-tipped cigarettes. She held them up in a V for victory or peace. A final declaration between us. Perhaps she knew this would be the end. Mom had been grilling my sister and me on the way home about our downstairs games ever since I mentioned the rubber penis. I heard her with

Dad, whispering the word *divorce*.

I waited for Elspeth to produce a lighter or a book of matches. Instead she bit the white part of the cigarette and began chewing, her eyes looking straight into mine as if swallowing a dare.

What are you doing? She bit off the rest. Her jaw moving like it was getting ready to leave her face. Bits of curly tobacco dangling at the corner of her mouth. Like a baby bird holding on to a last worm, unsure of its mother's return. Then her eyes began to water. *It's burning, my throat is burning.* She ran up the stairs without waiting for the sound of the timer.

After Mrs. Acker left Mr. Acker, we visited the department store and rarely found him there. It was eerie, as if someone had abandoned the helm. All those leather toes facing willy-nilly, soldiers lost on a field. He might as well have opened up the stockroom and hung a sign: TAKE WHATEVER FITS. That same year they discontinued the Buster Brown line at Eaton's and we had to go to a specialty store, where they measured every time, not just *knowing* like Mr. Acker. We had no reason to stop in.

BREAKUP FRESH

1.

It's Singles' Night at the museum. The taxi drops Dawn and
Tracy at the entrance. Tracy scowls at the families milling
about, the first-date couples with too-big smiles, taking
advantage of free-admission Friday.

A man in a suit leaps up the steps two at a time. He has
on a bowtie.

"Betcha he's going."

"Oh god," Dawn says.

"We're doing this," Tracy says firmly. "Three years of
celibacy's got to be enough to exorcise Ray from my man-
picking genome."

Dawn, ever the artist, is in black pigtails, gripping an

Andy Warhol purse. It's Campbell's Tomato Soup tonight, as opposed to Elvis gyrating across her bag. Doesn't want to be too suggestive. She's breakup fresh. Dawn's boyfriend, Christopher, converted to Sufism and asked her to move out three months ago.

They're ushered into the basement. The singles are all standing in an enclosed hexagonal space. Tracy thinks of beehives, drones dying in midair in the race to impregnate an aloof queen. She gives their names to two women behind the counter. They're younger than Dawn and Tracy, smiling a bit too much, too damn happy to be standing behind shoeboxes full of names that aren't theirs.

"Your name isn't on this confirmation slip," says one of them. "You paid online? You needed to print out the other part."

Tracy is about to tell Dawn she needs to go home to print out the other part. But they let them in anyway, handing over plasticized clip-on nametags with a computer graphic of a martini glass — half empty, no olive.

"Oh god," Tracy says, as they enter the hive room. They hover around a table of crackers and white cheese cubes the size of cheap engagement diamonds. They step towards a table of pink punch glasses, two gay waiters serving.

"I can't do this without booze, Tracy," Dawn whispers. "Is there booze in this?" she asks.

"Oh no, that's later." The waiters laugh like kindergarten teachers regulating snack time. There's no chance to get angry with them. The girls are herded into the theatre, where Tracy now sees the three-to-one ratio of women to men. An elderly man stands behind a podium, saying that he can hardly contain his excitement that they are all there.

"He's probably calculating forty-four dollars times all us fools," Dawn says.

The title of the slide lecture is "Get the Girl." A tall, sexy woman over fifty, with long silver hair, delivers a talk on the advice men have been given since antiquity regarding the opposite sex. Wooing, pleasing, potions, rituals, magic words. She boils it all down to a few words of wisdom: above all else, give her whatever she wants.

A man in a Hawaiian shirt and shorts sitting beside Tracy comments on every image presented on the screen. "Looks like a vibrator to me." Then, "Begging always works." Tracy snickers at each comment. After all, the ticket says "Singles *Social*." She needs to at least try. But she stares straight ahead because he is the only audience member talking and she doesn't want to encourage him. The one time she looks at him, Tracy sees he's at least twenty years her senior. She stops snickering.

The anthropologist flicks her hair a lot, which, combined with her partially exposed cleavage and occasional naughty word, seems to be working for most of the men in the audience. "Good luck," she says, her fist high in the air as if sending troops off to battle, and then they're corralled in the next room. The one with the free glass of wine. For this they must pass through the museum, past the screaming, haggard mothers and strolling Friday-night couples.

Tracy suddenly longs for her green leather couch with its big poofy arms, Nina Simone on her IPod, three bookmarked novels with female protagonists who wouldn't dream of attending Singles' Night.

"Let's ditch," she says to Dawn.

"What about the free wine?"

Just then Tracy hears someone say, "Free tickets for Jane Siberry."

They slip out of their martini'd-nametag line and get two tickets from a museum attendant. One of the Singles' organizers quickly manoeuvres them back into line, but they pat the tickets in their pockets.

They go through the sky-high red curtains into the museum hall, disguised as a grand ballroom. It's full of men older than time. Everyone holds a green bingo card with squares that say things like FIND SOMEONE WHO HAS RECENTLY GONE ON A TRIP or FIND SOMEONE WHO IS ALLERGIC TO SOMETHING. Tracy is deathly allergic to seafood. No one approaches them to ask.

"I am deathly allergic to seafood," she tells the waiter. He disappears to ask about the hors d'oeuvres and never returns. They stand in the grand hall, downing their white wine. Men are approaching women. All around them men and women are laughing, scratching names on bingo cards. The girls think maybe they're too young. Too funky. Too intimidating.

Or maybe the men can smell something about them. In one of the squares Tracy writes *allergic to fish: ME* and deposits her card in some box for a draw before they slip back out into the museum.

Tracy and Dawn stand in the doorway to the hall, listening to Jane Siberry. Men and women closer to their age sit tapping their toes, jackets slung over the backs of their folding chairs. Jane's standing on a low stage close to the crowd, wearing a blue, blue dress, blond hair in tight knots all over her head like a sturdy net. She plays her guitar and sings a song about sitting in a boat on the water, before the beginning of time. The moment before. The moment before possibility. *Not yet, not yet.* The words travel down Tracy's spine and back up, sting out her eyes. She tries not to look at Dawn, because if she moves, the water will move.

Jane stops playing her guitar. All goes silent. She whispers into the mike, "Are you ready? All you need to do is let go. Are you ready?"

2.

Ray finally said "I love you." In bed, in the room next to Tracy's parents' bedroom. It was his first time meeting them, being in their big house by the highway. She had been saying the words for weeks. Telling him love is not a promise, just a feeling.

It was dark and she couldn't see his face. He said it twice. Then, "Should I turn on the light so you can see me say it?"

The lamp was too far from the bed. "No," she said.

She knew it was because he liked the house, its huge, quiet riches, how everything stood still, the high-backed dining chairs, the marble chess set.

She misses him the way one misses a perpetually dying plant on the windowsill. He watched her breeze in and out to piano lessons, choir meetings, drum classes. Like he was breathing for the first time. His dark face suddenly open, standing at the door to their apartment. The way a father watches a daughter get ready for her first recital. She kept adding things to her list. To impress him. To keep him grounded there, struck by her energy. When they went out, he placed his hand strongly on her back, ushering her towards his friends so he could brag about her life. The more she grew, the skinnier he appeared, the more he wore black. Sophisticated, she thought. Until his fists tightened, his words eroding her musical abilities, the possibility of a life separate from him.

She sees him only in her dreams now. Coming through the forest for her. Like the Big Bad Wolf. She's disappointed, because she's just finished decorating herself a house that suits her every need, her heart finally content. In her dreams Ray kicks her in the stomach and they have makeup sex stronger than mortar. She knows there will never be another like this. The depth of it. The tears. The repulsion and the coming back to herself as she rides him, making those animal noises. So that even the Woodcutter, ambling through the woods, holds still, wondering if it's pain or pleasure he's hearing. But he is busy with another wolf, another story. And in her dream she is never rescued; she simply moves house, leaves the neighbourhood. Gets her phone number unlisted. And every time Ray finds her, she sighs and opens the door before he breaks it down.

She'd like to say Ray didn't destroy her. She'd like to omit that part of her romantic history, but that would be cutting out the thing every girl dreams of. Heathcliff on the moor. Confessions of girls well into the wine: *the best sex we've ever had*. With each new first date she keeps Ray like a medal, like a hard-earned Brownie badge sewn onto her sash that she will choose to show at the right moment. When she smells that a man needs a little something in her to bandage. When she can think of no other reason for him to stay.

3.

The speed-dating event is the following week. Tracy's committed. Since the museum night it's all about momentum, but she knows Dawn's losing steam. A flat waterfall cascades behind the bar. The bartender smiles conspiratorially as Tracy asks for a double rum and Coke.

"Me too," Dawn says.

"I feel like James Bond on a new mission."

Tracy notices the up-and-down eyes of the men as each new woman comes in. Their nervous sipping of drinks, standing together but not close enough to collapse the air of competition. All safe in their dark suits or casual dress pants, newly laundered shirts. Most of the women look tired, a few steps into middle age, decked out in their sexiest outfits, ten years past hip. The bulge where control-top pantyhose end, a new push-up bra, hair desperate for conditioner. Gina and Toni — "hostesses" for the evening — tell everyone to sit at one of the alphabetically marked tables. Tracy chooses the one in the corner, a tiny U next to a tea light. Dawn is three spots over, at R. Every three minutes, at the sound of a small bell, the men move to a new table.

From where she is sitting, Tracy can see the whole room. The crossed legs of the women. The way the men hike up their belts as they move between "dates." She can see Dawn but they avoid eye contact, knowing they will start to giggle. Tracy doesn't want the men getting paranoid. She wants to see them at their best.

They are all given a list with numbers corresponding to their nametags, and each time she hears the bell, Tracy finds herself in a frantic moment of shaking hands and "It was very nice to meet you . . . What was your number again?" Each man pushes out his chest for her to read and she curls up her paper like it's a math exam. She even tries to disguise the motion of her wrist making an X in the No column.

It isn't that she doesn't think any of them worthy of a Yes, but in her panic and indecision she finds herself playing it safe. Maybe it's the question she's chosen; it isn't giving her enough to go on. Dawn and Tracy brainstormed for weeks, bounced samples off friends. Tracy decided to make her question multiple choice. Books: Grisham, Tolstoy, or Ellis? Movies: Fellini, Jet Li, or Michael Moore? Papers: *Star*, *Sun*, or *Globe*? Dawn's going with hangers: wire, wood, or plastic?

But when the first man sat down, Tracy found herself saying, "What's the most interesting question you've been asked so far?"

"Well, there was this one about hangers. I said 'wood' and she seemed happy with that." And, "There was this weird one about wire." In this way Tracy discovers how things are going for Dawn while piggybacking on her question. One man explains his preference for all three materials and his system of what each is used for. Another goes on to describe his wooden shoetrees that absorb sweat at night. Yet another — this one cufflinked and spice-cologned — steps over her question and firmly plants his own: "How many hangers are in your closet?"

"Not enough," she answers. Later, when she receives her list of matches via email and sees he hasn't chosen her, Tracy realizes this was not the correct answer. The night has been all about correct answers.

At the break, Dawn needs a smoke. The shortest guy

follows them outside. Pops a Nicorette gum in his mouth.

"You girls first-timers? This is my second time. I got this one free. If you don't get a match, you get the next one free. It's fun, though. I've met lots of nice people." He keeps running his hand through his hair. Tracy remembers this is one of the things criminals do when cops ask where they've hidden the money. When he heads to the washroom, she says, "Some guys are devoid of sexuality."

"You know, I've been thinking about how I can get back at Chris," Dawn says.

Tracy's proud of Dawn. She's done pretty well, talking to all those guys for one and a half hours about hangers instead of about Christopher.

"I'm thinking of doing a public art display. Plaster the telephone poles in his neighbourhood with posters of whirling dervishes. The caption would say something like 'Whirling in Self-Love,' or 'Screwing Someone Over in the Name of Allah.' That's the Sufi god. But I'd have to put the posters right outside his apartment; otherwise he'll never notice them. I think that would really freak him out."

After the break Tracy sees from Dawn's body language at the R table that she's given up. Arms crossed, leaning way back, probably shooting sarcasm in a so-not-available tone. The Warhol soup can in a crushed heap beside her hip.

Tracy decides on a new question. "What are you fanatical about?" The responses are varied. "My car. It's a '69 Charger. Remember *The Dukes of Hazzard*? The General Lee? I've been fixing it up for ten years. It's lime green. The engine's perfect. I drive it every weekend."

"Sex, of course."

"Life. I love life." Tracy notices that this grey-haired

man sits sideways in the chair like he has an appointment to go to. His hand makes circles as if spinning a Rolodex. "I ski. I snowboard. I play tennis, squash. I scuba dive. I swim. I run. I cycle."

Some don't wait for Tracy's question. "Right. Okay, I'm forty-two. Happily divorced. One child. Lives with me every other weekend. I don't smoke and I work in film and video."

Before long Tracy begins to feel her optimism slip beneath the table, her limbs getting very heavy. As if the lists these men have given her are something she will have to clean up later. Bags of hockey equipment, piles of laundry growing around her feet. The ones who've never married, never had kids, have shiny faces that Tracy can't see into. They seem to say, *I can withstand this for three minutes.* As the night wears on, Tracy is no longer seeing the presentation, the slick suit, the witty banter. It is their dark guard; the eyes she knows will eventually ask her to hold their pain.

By the last four, she's switched to asking, "So, have you ever been in prison?" She feels herself floating above the table, like the bride in a Chagall painting. One hand clinging tenuously to the male on the ground, the other hand holding her wedding bouquet of hope.

4.

Every night it happens. This miraculous thing. Just before dinner. Tracy lies on the green couch with her book, feels the light entering. She looks up at her living room wall to watch the sun creep around the corner of her apartment building. The horizontal lines of her blinds spread their perfect silhouette, progressing towards her on the couch. At some point she thinks she catches the shadows growing.

It is as if the wall is lit from within, exposing some hidden musical staff. The shadow of her candlesticks on the table a cryptic time signature.

The geranium, which has far outgrown its tiny pot, is heading up the wall. The green heads of each stem, not yet in bloom, form a perfectly placed chord. The tallest reaches high C. She watches the ends of the light between the dark slats on her wall, the embossing of a five-line staff.

Tonight they go past the midway point of her sofa's first cushion. And then the light brightens nearest the window. A signal. *Are you ready?* And just as she thinks she will finally see a whole row of geraniums across the staff in quarter-note code, it's gone. Like an invisible-ink message held too close to the candle, it's gone. Fallen back, spent, into the blue of her walls. *Not yet, not yet.*

SACRIFICE

Didi hauls that army duffle bag all through Tibet. Calls it Bradley. It's as tall as she is. Stuffed like a sherry trifle, one-third clothes, one-third books, and later, when I have a wicked cold in one of the many hellhole towns in China, she shows me the bottom third. Herbal teas, hot water bottle, grape-flavoured cough drops, cashews, dried mango. The Elgin Marbles of her upscale London life. Her father is a world-renowned composer, a fact she shares only with me, knowing that the rest of our group will not have heard of him. As a child, at one of her father's many lavish parties, she hung a sheet of paper on the bathroom door before climbing into bed in her pyjamas: PLEASE SIGN HERE IF YOU'RE FAMOUS. She awoke to *Leonard Bernstein*.

The dozen of us come from various parts of the world,

all having read the same Adventure Travel brochure. On the second night Didi and I share a damp floral-bedspreaded room. Two Chinese women knock on the door, tuck us both in tight, and leave a red Thermos full of hot water to splash under our arms. Unable to move, we begin imitating our fellow travellers, complete with accents.

Okay, who's this? *Look, there's a chicken.*

Joan! Okay, who's this? *Don't they have anything besides rice?*

Maritha!

With this we become permanent roomies for the two weeks as our Jeep convoy springs its way across the rocky plateau.

I observe Didi as she scans tables full of sacred trinkets in Buddhist markets, her chestnut hair curtaining her face. Her fingers reaching emphatically, devouring inscribed discs. Although we're the same age, she answers my questions with questions ending in "little one." On the buses and trucks she curls up against the window with a small red book, closes it quickly when I ask to read it too.

Buddhist texts can't be read until one is ready, she says. You won't understand them, dear.

What's the harm, then? I say.

One needs a teacher, a monk who regulates knowledge. To be exposed too early can cause great damage. Let's see what Bradley has for you. Didi speaks like a proper English nanny.

At our hotel she unknots the drawstring and pulls out *Moby Dick*, Homer's *Odyssey*, Chekhov, Tolstoy, Kafka. This is the one for you, she says. Thomas Mann's *Magic Mountain* drops on the bed.

She lugs Bradley in and out of every truck and bus, infuriating our tour guide. At night she writes the real Bradley long letters, notebook on her knees, tenting the blanket to look like the Afghani mountains where he is on assignment.

He's in the north now, she says. How he got in, I haven't a clue. No one gets into the north. He says not to expect any correspondence for a while. I'm beginning to think he's not a journalist at all. Bradley could very well be a spy.

At 3 a.m. I head to the lobby in ski jacket and pyjamas, find the hotel attendant asleep on a couch. He watches me dial my boyfriend, Nick. The receiver heavy, clunky, like the Bat Phone.

I tell Nick we travel 200 kilometres each day, sometimes climbing as high as 6,700 metres. I've never seen such a blue sky, I say. There's prayer flags with horses on them, and *chortens* — piles of rocks — everywhere, like little men dancing at the high passes.

I can hear that a British accent has crept into my words.

He says he's learning about carburetors and thinks he knows what that sputter is in my Toyota. He's got three more courses to go, and Sam might offer him an apprenticeship.

I love you, I say, because I want a Bradley too.

Didi knows without my saying that I have picked the farthest place from home. My Canadian-flagged backpack. Every day we pile into the Jeeps, I hold tight to *The Magic Mountain*. Didi and I up front with Surnam, whose pink shirt is eternally clean, his suit jacket over the back of his seat. He looks at the book, shakes his head and laughs, wraps his puffy fingers around the steering wheel. His thumbprints large, like tree rings. The Jeep rearranges my internal organs, roads disappear into streams, and I look down at the switchback we've climbed through the mountains, like a stick trailed through sand. I'm desperately, unsuccessfully marking where I've come.

Then long stretches of flatland, fields of stone, an occasional patch of yellow barley like thinning hair. We come to a valley, another monastery. The same cluster of white cube buildings, rooftops and window frames the colour of dried blood. We've read that thousands of monks were killed by the Chinese army. Buildings destroyed during the revolution linger beside rebuilds, and the few monks we see seem like ghosts. Tucked into our underwear, just as the guidebooks advised, are outlawed pictures of the Dalai Lama. Tibetans in fedoras ride past on horseback, nomads in green army coats, long black braids wrapped around their heads in 108 criss-crosses, the number of sutras they have to recite. On every main street we roll into there's a pool table or two, someone asleep on the green felt in the afternoon sun.

When I say I'm too tired to wash my face or clean my teeth at the end of each day, Didi says, We mustn't forgo that which makes us feel human. In Bongda, Didi and I find a courtyard with windows boarded up, and a hose. We hold a towel up for one another, our pink soap washing away the week, our hair taking three rinses to flatten it wet against our scalps. Above all, be impeccable, she says.

Didi is impeccable. Her long hair up in a curl of a bun, a white silk scarf wrapped three times round her neck like a string of pearls. I watch her lips purse when someone says something that makes her cringe. As we sit on the bus in this arid, deforested landscape, the polluted Yangtze going in the opposite direction, I come to see each person's internal landscape through Didi's eyes.

Abby, the hairdresser, who's lost half her weight from eating only rice, admits to spending all her time picturing the moment her boyfriend sees her at the airport in the skin-tight blouse she had custom-made in Dali. The variety of sexual positions to be practised in their East London apartment, amongst the Buddhas and floor-to-ceiling Chinese scrolls she's purchased, unsure of their meaning.

Alfred scans the roadside for blue poppies, screaming *Stop* when he sees a tiny white flower with three petals, native to New Zealand. From the window we watch him huddle over something visible only to him. He tells us the Latin names of things; the last words of his sentences deteriorate into a chuckle.

Mats and Maritha from Denmark are on their pre-university round-the-world trip, paid for by Daddy. They hoard bags of babi bread and apples, complaining about Tsingtao beer, searching for candy stalls to supplement the untouched orders of french fries. They just don't taste potatoey enough, Maritha says. Look at the banana pancakes, they're just slices on top.

Eric sees Tibet through a huge telephoto lens, taking ten photos to each of our one. This cold is nothing; it gets to fifty below in Edmonton, he says each morning. Joan feels compelled to ask, What's that? at every turn, as if things don't exist until labelled. Madhur, a grief-stricken freshly divorced Brit, starts sleeping with our leader, Jack, and spends most of the trip orienting herself to him, her tops progressively holding less of her breasts.

Jack is Didi's antithesis. The Aussie guide who underfeeds us with bowel-congesting meals of Spam and Tibetan noodles. When hotels become scarce, he produces tents unfit for sub-zero temperatures, tin pegs that fold when we hammer them into the frozen plateau. We awaken to wet sleeping bags and the water solid in our bottles. He says, Don't bother with anti-malarials. I've had it three times. It's just a high fever and a week or two in hospital. After a lot of barley beer one night, he tells us he makes money on every tour by skimming part of the food kitty, and says there's something bewitching about Madhur and her brown skin.

We trade in our Jeeps for one minibus for the day trip to Degen. I begin wearing a scarf like Didi's, pulling it up over my chin for comfort when the roads get narrow. Stare nervously at Didi's side of the bus, the two-thousand-metre drop to the Yangtze. That's when I see her first sacrifice. She's holding a can of Spam on the edge of the open window. Taken from one of Jack's lazily planned lunches. Absentmindedly rubbing it along the edge. Her aviator sunglasses and her topknot give her the look of a praying mantis, the bug that rips off its lover's head after sex. She looks at me, then lets it go. From my seat across the aisle I am the only witness.

You did that on purpose, I say.

Later our hotel costs one yuan, or five American dollars. It is a prison cell of rolled-up stained mattresses on iron cots. Children call through our barred window most of the night.

Sacrifice, Didi tells me, is focused primarily on improving one's chances for a more favourable life in the future. With the Spam offering we invite more nutritious food, she says. She asks me to think of the next one. A *kata*, the white scarf we've seen in temples, wrapped around the many hands of Avalokitesvara. A *kata* belonging to Joan. When the nun in Zhong Dian laid it over her shoulders, Joan said, I'll use that as a cover for my TV stand; my maple laminate's all scratched up.

Didi and I get up early, eat dumplings, and start out ahead of the group on the windy road towards the cliff monastery, Drigung Till. It's snowed during the night. We walk past staring yaks, a lonely shepherd who calls, *Tashi dele*. We start to worry; it's three and a half hours and still no sign of the Jeeps. A woman appears in a long aproned skirt and fur-lined coat, sleeves almost to her knees, a baby with rosy cheeks tucked in her hood. She offers us tea and we begin to make alternative plans: living with the locals, hitching to Lhasa. We watch her hoist her skirt, pee in the cold. Drigung? we ask, thinking the Jeeps are lost and we'll have to find our way up the mountain. She points behind us to the white and burgundy building clinging to the cliffside. We missed the fork in the road, too busy talking about Jack to bother looking up.

He doesn't even have a guidebook, Didi. Did you hear him ask Madhur if he could photocopy those pages on Sera Monastery?

Expect nothing and you'll never be disappointed.

I'm so bunged up from all the frigging Spam. You'd think he'd pick up some food at the markets, but no, he's too busy trying to get into Madhur's pants.

There's a perfect example of attachment leading to suffering. The only reason she lowers herself is because she doesn't know who she is right now. She's looking more and more shell-shocked.

Thank god you forced him to buy those blankets in town when we were camping. I mean, come on, did he not know the tents were crap? I thought he'd done Tibet before.

Let's write a letter to Travel Adventures. We can fax it when we get to Nepal.

It's a nerve-wracking half-hour back to the turnoff, knowing we may have missed the Jeeps. I start bargaining in my head with Vajrapani, the conqueror of negativity with his thunderbolt of compassion. It works — we get picked up soon after.

At Drigung two dozen curly-tailed dogs, rumoured to be reincarnated monks, doze on the stone terrace. Red-robed boys appear in doorways wearing running shoes, hold up handfuls of yak butter. A snowball fight breaks out in the courtyard, the youngsters' arms naked, biceps reminiscent of Major League pitchers. Two monks are doing laundry, bare feet massaging burgundy cloth on the stones, steaming hot water bleeding down the steps. They smile.

A bell rings. The boys run in; we follow. The long rows of red cushions we've seen empty in monasteries across Tibet here hold cross-legged bodies, all busy arranging their robes. Some with long, rectangular books — sutras — open on their laps. They sway and chant. The head monk on an elevated cushion, eyes closed, his hands carving the air like an Indian dancer's, occasionally rings a tiny bell. The rows of monks chant, sometimes raising their hands in unison to echo his movements, but mostly they stare at us as we walk around the hall, sit near them. One monk moves down the line, filling cups with yak-butter tea.

I watch a monk near the front of the hall make balls of barley. He drops them in a small dish, pours oil from his kettle until they float. When it overflows, a monk with a perfectly round head dumps the *tsampa* balls and the contents of the dish. He works on five dishes at a time; sometimes, instead of a ball, he forms a cone. The ball is the body, the cone is the head, Didi explains. Body and mind, united by breath, she says, but I don't really understand. They remain on the altar for a week, she says. The old ones are given to the dogs.

Didi stands quietly against a wall while the rest of our group moves in and out of the rows, cameras poised. I think to tuck my Pentax inside my ski jacket and join her, but the doors swing open. Two huge nomads with sun-worn faces stand in the entrance, clasp their hands in *namaste*, then drop to the floor in full prostration again and again. The blue sky behind. They have travelled by foot with yaks and tents and babies. I can't help it — I take the photo.

After Drigung, Didi seems driven to concentrate on the sacrifices. We brainstorm together, but sometimes an unexpected object appears unattended. Didi decides I'm the better "taker." She composes rhyming couplets to be recited at the moment of sacrifice. *Joan, whose mouth makes us tired, take this kata and leave her mired.* We offer up Madhur's bra at a high pass, tie it with the flapping prayer flag as nomads circumambulate the stupa. Abby's homecoming thong makes a fine donation to the river as our Jeep follows the submerged road. Didi and I looking the other way while Eric photographs a woman bathing. His Canon fisheye lens finds a home in the turquoise lake Yamdrok Yumtso. A tent pole of Mats', a bag of Maritha's chewy candy. Surnam, who regularly scans our chests while driving, loses his red tartan Thermos. We await a better future.

We are camping on the plateau, a beautiful spot by the river. Didi and I prepare for a full strip-down bathe. A truck, the kind we've seen all across the plateau, painted blue with a metal lotus over the cab, pulls up with about forty men standing in the back. Didi and I huddle inside our tent, hear the engine cut, boots running around the campsite, loud cheers. Footsteps and voices come suddenly close, then fall silent. We see the tent zipper rise. Four huge faces stare at us as if we are unfound treasures. We're holding our breath.

Dalai Lama, Dalai Lama, they chant, and Didi reaches into her track pants and offers a photo of the fourteenth lama, in exile since 1959, taken from a London newspaper. They snatch it out of her hand and run off cheering. Didi peeks out. They are tearing around to pose wherever Eric points his lens.

Finally we hear the truck start up and pull away. Pudun, our guide, is furious. On a recent trip a tourist gave out two Dalai Lama pictures and the villagers showed them around. Within two days the police had caught up with the trip and took the tourist to Lhasa for a flight out. The tour director lost his licence.

Didi, however, is not sorry. She's angry with Jack. Those men could have done anything to us, she tells me. Who do you think would protect us? Jack? Alfred? Eric? They were too bloody busy getting their damn photos. And where was Pudun?

She confronts Jack and he says it's all right, everything was under control. They even helped us with our tents, he says. He shows her his Swiss army knife as proof of protection, as if it could even begin to compete with their Tibetan knives.

It's our final sacrifice, that knife, along with one of Jack's shoes. For clomping ignorantly across this Buddhist land, not knowing what stupas are, or dharma wheels, or even the butter and *tsampa* sculptures we see on all the altars.

At Lalung-La Pass Joan is the first to call out, Look, Mount Everest. It's actually Mount Qomolangma, Didi says, sounding angry. The bus parks. The air is thin. The whole group climbs the loose stones like a pack of moon men, taking giant, slow steps with laboured breaths. The wind almost pushing us back. Piles of *mani* stones, *chorten*s like dwarves pointing to the rooftop of the world. There's a podium showing the four mountains: Qomolangma, Makara, Lhoze, and Cho Oyo. And a stele that says PEACE EVERLASTING ON EARTH.

When we get to the crest, we take photos. It's just like the posters, Joan says, and goes back to sit in the warmth of the bus. No one wants to have lunch in that wind. We wait for Didi. I watch her begin to dance there on the hill, amongst the pebbles previous travellers have piled into wobbly figures. She's alluded to studying Gurdjieff, and I see her as a whirling dervish, taller than the surrounding stone followers. I should be out there with her.

We're a few days away from the end of the tour in Kathmandu. I realize I've been waiting to go home since I arrived. I've been cleaning up Asia, thinking, *If they just straightened up their yards, tidied the rubbish spilling down the hill into the Yangtze, righted a mailbox, replaced an industrial roll-down door with a beautiful wooden one. If Asia just had curb appeal.* I scold myself for not sitting longer in front of the altars, the gold avatars, the long rows of round pillows in the dim, high-ceilinged rooms. For not feeling anchored. I take photos of monks, thinking, *I'll look at them when I get home.*

We drive twenty kilometres back down the road to reacclimatize, looking at a brown landscape. Didi has tears rolling down her cheeks, I assume because the moment has been cut short. She shakes her head no, she doesn't want to talk.

The Magic Mountain, page 239, finally corresponds with the journey. I record the quote in my journal. *Waiting means hurrying on ahead, it means regarding time and the present moment not as a boon, but an obstruction; it means making their actual content null and void, by mentally overlapping them. Waiting, we say, is long. We might just as well — or more accurately — say it's short, since it consumes whole spaces of time without our living them.*

It's our last night in Tibet. We're at the Hotel Everest View, although the mountain is nowhere to be seen. Didi says she's meeting Bradley in India. She'll fly there from Kathmandu. She says Calcutta is like a second home; her brother works with orphans there. When I ask her about it, she clams up. When Jack asks if anyone's seen a brown loafer, she smirks briefly, then sticks her nose in her book.

He has been buying fireworks all along the journey. Our rooms encircle a huge courtyard. The group stands along the upper balcony, waiting for the show. Didi and I stay inside our room, watching from the window. It's dark, but every few minutes we see a tiny light, then the explosion illuminates Jack's figure running, for a slight second, running for his life.

By candlelight we compose the letter like two girls writing a story. I want to call him Dumdum Jack, but Didi supplies a large vocabulary to describe insufficient camping equipment, extreme food rationing, and Jack's confession of stolen funds. We struggle with how to describe Jack's obsession with Madhur, and in the end write: *He began fucking one of the women early on in the tour.* My name alone goes on the letter. Didi says she can't sign it because she is associated with Tibetan freedom groups, and it may put her in danger to have her whereabouts in Nepal known. I don't think to question her.

In the middle of the night I have to pee. I resist as long as I can. It's freezing, and I put on my ski jacket to cross the courtyard and climb two sets of concrete stairs to a room with two holes in the floor. I squat, avoid looking down. The moon is strong, and I look up to the tiny square window high in the wall.

There it is. Mount Everest, perfectly framed. Its jagged white tip 3-D against an indigo sky. *Wait till I tell Didi*, I think. *She'll chuckle at this.* I stay squatting for a while, the only person awake in all of Tibet, communing with the mountain. The frame disappears. In the morning I look at Didi doggedly packing Bradley, the knob of bun bobbing like a line sinker, and I don't say anything.

The group is booked to stay in the Nepal Guest House but Didi and I have reserved a room for two in the famous Kathmandu Guest House, facing out on the peaceful Buddha Garden. We plan to present Jack with the letter, then disappear to our hotel, avoiding the gang's farewell dinner at the Hard Yak Cafe.

When we arrive in the room, we throw down our bags and Didi crawls into bed in her clothes. A stomach ache, she says, and I leave her there with the pigeons cooing loudly on the windowsill. I head to the post office to fax the letter. I walk through the meandering streets, avoiding rickshaws and hawkers whispering, Change money? Pot? Tiger Balm? Seeing all the comforts of home: cappuccino, pizza, hamburgers.

I get back to find Didi isn't there. I know she's really gone because Bradley is gone too. I ask at the desk. There's a note. *I'm at the Nepal Guest House.* Magic Mountain *is yours to keep.*

I head to the lobby to phone Nick, planning to meet him somewhere exotic, like Thailand. One of the islands, maybe Phuket or Ko Pi Pi. We'll rent a bungalow on stilts, canopied by lush trees. It will be too hot to move, except from our door to the beach. We'll wade for miles through the placid green water and it will still only come to our knees. It's three in the morning in Toronto. I know he'll talk about air filters and fan belts and rusty brake pads. That he won't be able to get away from his studies. He too is learning how things work.

I think of how, in the first week of our trip through Vietnam, before Didi and I hooked up, the group visited the car of the Buddhist monk Thich Quang Duc. He burned himself to death at a busy intersection on June 11, 1963, in protest of the persecution of Buddhists by the South Vietnamese government. After his death his body was re-cremated, but his heart remained, unable to burn.

This is true sacrifice, I wrote in my journal. Several pages later I wrote about the Naxi women of Lijiang, one of the few matriarchies in the world. They all dress in dark blue blouses and blazers, carrying tall baskets on their backs. They are free to take a lover without living with him. Children stay with the mother, requiring male support only for as long as the relationship lasts. Women inherit all property, female elders oversee disputes, and in the Naxi language, if the word for *female* is added, it increases the heft of the word. *Stone* plus *female* equals *boulder*. *Stone* plus *male* equals *pebble*.

Beside this entry I now sketch Didi as a huge rock. I think of the day in front of Mount Everest. I pocketed a tiny *mani* stone from one of the stacks. Didi was furious, saying I didn't understand the significance. I sketch that stack of rubble, plus Bradley, me, and all future pebbles. A precarious *chorten* on some bleak promenade, awaiting further instructions.

NOT ENOUGH FOR ME, SIR

1.

Water bottles weren't allowed. Coffee cups, okay. And you could fill them with water. But the bottle was considered a trigger. If Emily saw the bottle she'd feel she should be drinking water too. Keeping her stomach liquid-full so the food would never have a chance to be absorbed. Peeing lots. Then she'd be near the porcelain bowl, a trigger for her fingers to get into her throat quick. There were no locks on the washroom doors at the Eating Disorder Clinic. If Emily said she had to go pee, Nancy would answer with one eyebrow up. Like the request was attached to a timer and it was ticking.

Last week the topic was distraction. If you get the urge,

she said, you have to put something between you and the behaviour. Like a wedge in a door. The wedge they called delay, and it was supposed to be a miracle. Like it would snip the connection and you'd forget to binge or purge or run to the gym. But Emily knew as soon as she hit a bump, she'd be back cruising the supermarket bakery, so why even start?

That day Emily was the first to arrive for Symptom Interruption Group at Sick Kids. It's one of those teaching hospitals: *I agree to be observable and research-worthy at all times.* In the room, eight seats were arranged in a circle, as usual. But there was a plate of cupcakes, buns, and pastries on the low table where they usually put their weekly food diaries. Emily's brain snatched the chocolate cake and shoved it in her mouth before she could put the wedge in the door. Luckily her hand had heard the part about delay. Then she saw the broccoli floret, the chicken breast, the heap of corn kernels. Plastic. All rubbery plastic. Today's topic: portion size. Now she remembered.

She sat near the window. It was sunset, the time Emily usually lay on her bed watching the light fill her apartment, knowing her day had officially ended because she'd consumed all her calories. The walls and carpet would turn orange or white yellow. She figured dying was like that. A whole room of light and you walking into it.

"Hey, Emily." She saw Carey scan the food as she put her bag down on the chair next to Emily.

"Hi."

"Ohmygod, I thought it was real!" Carey squealed. Emily smiled like she'd known right away it wasn't. Carey took off her coat. *She always wears the same jeans,* Emily thought. The tight ones that tell you immediately if you've gained weight. Tight right to the ankles. Like Carey was watching those too. Hooker pumps so she could feel her hips when she walked, Emily figured, remember her sex even though she was so far from it. Last week she'd told them her periods had stopped a few years ago, when she was twenty-two. Carey held a coffee cup. Emily bet her ass it was water. Carey's fingernails were long and red, probably so she could admire them clutching all those negative calories, catch herself being good. Although Emily had recently learned that water has calories, she knew it was like a janitor swishing his mop through the bowels saying, *All right, everybody get the hell out.*

Emily looked at her own bitten nails, the way her thighs almost touched the arms of the chair. Carey's ass took up a third of her seat. Emily knew Carey measured because she kind of rocked side to side in the chair, hips hitting the space like an NHLer stickhandling.

That's how it was. You had to be ready, Emily thought, for what life would dish out. And being ready meant being thin.

Liz came in next. Tall and Swiss like a cuckoo-clock doll. Curly black hair, face wide like a plant determined to grow towards the light. The lint collector in the corner, clogged to capacity. Whatever happened there, they all knew they could at least deflect it onto her.

"Hi, everyone." This time it was Nancy. Eating-disorder expert. Not a spot of too fat or too thin on her. Part of the I-Love-My-Body Club. She too held supposed coffee, but in a Thermos.

When the chairs were all filled, she said, "Let's check

in." After four weeks in this group Emily knew they were all liars. Truth only came out the way stuffing pokes its way out of an old couch. Except for maybe Liz, who always told the truth, but she was crazy. With her the truth changed so fast, Emily couldn't keep up.

Carey went first. "I'm okay."

Liar, Emily said, not out loud.

"My goal last week was five purges a day. I did that for two days, but the rest were more. I don't want to say the actual number." Her eyes darted around the group but her mouth moved slowly. Partly because her bottom jaw was protruding. Her top teeth rotting out because of all the stomach acid. "And I said I was going to spend no more than fifty dollars a day on binges. But I didn't meet that goal. I had a hard week because my hairdresser says my hair — right here — is falling out." She touched the top of her head like a priest performing a christening, slow and gentle, but Emily knew that didn't match what was inside her. "And I've taken so many laxatives that my muscles . . ." Her long red fingernail pointed towards her jeans. "Well, my intestines are coming down and I kind of have to push them back up."

Too much! Emily screamed inwardly. *I'm twenty-nine. I've spent way too much time on this already.*

Emily was next. "I only exercised three times this week. The other four days I just did my sit-ups and push-ups, but on the days I didn't go to the gym, I didn't binge. I guess because I knew I couldn't get it off me. But you know what happened on those days? The hate got louder. I hated my body. I hated everyone at work who said, 'Try harder. Do better.' I hated men. More than I usually do. It was just like, *I give up. Fuck off. I can't be what you want me to be, okay?*"

Nancy nodded with sad empathic eyes.

Liz was next. She hadn't taken her meds. Nancy gave her shit. Emily figured Liz was bipolar, because some weeks she reported how many hours she had spent at the gym and how many universities she had applied to, her face expecting a prize from the group. Today her check-in went on forever. "My mother won't let me blah blah blah . . . She says I'm blah blah blah . . . and my boss hates me and everyone's trying to blah blah blah . . ." She let the tears come down throughout, her hands moving only to blot the streaming mascara.

Nancy tried to cut her off, even though she wasn't supposed to interrupt check-in. Emily saw Nancy losing it. She said, "What does the group think about Liz's exercising? How does the group feel about what Liz is saying? Could someone say something to Liz?"

Nancy was giving up, like the geranium in Emily's apartment. For months it had been growing tall and narrow, neck straining to stay upright. Emily knew she needed to repot it, but she knew she wouldn't. When the time came, she would just throw it out and buy a new one. That morning she had awakened to find it flopped over. What she had thought was its only stalk had secretly grown into two, and now the stems were bent over in opposite directions. It was an entirely different plant, wide, sprawling along the hardwood. Making decisions without her.

She looked at the group leader's coffee cup. It appeared to Emily as clear plastic now; she could see right through. The judgement, the anger, the self-love and lies, all swirling black bits from a bad filter. Emily knew that as soon as she left there she would go to the gym. The set course of things just goes on. Like wind whistling through the space of a wedged-open door.

2.

Six months later, Emily sat with Hayley in Hugh's Room. Hayley all pinked up, fluffy sweater tight, breasts round as her flushed cheeks. Emily doing all black. Trying to pretend she didn't still have a few pounds to lose. Both trying not to let anything say, *Secretaries at the end of a shit week.* They had paid ten dollars to see a band called the Silver Lockets. Knew it might be hard to get their money's worth from a band with a name like that. Sat at the table near the entrance, flowers turning their faces to the sun. Red lips buzzing.

Turned out the band had eleven members. Turned out it was okay. They wore second-hand suits. One played the trombone. Another, a really long harmonica. The one standing at the back wore a bowtie. Playing the accordion like it was cool. Emily silently chose the skinniest, the one with the ostrich face and red hair. From where they were sitting they could see his left hand moving through the air, playing an invisible keyboard framed by steel rods. The hand looked like it was locked in a guitar strum. His other arm permanently up, saying, *Hey, wait a minute.* Like lightning had struck and he was bent over listening for damage. They realized he was responsible for turning every song into a *Twin Peaks* soundtrack.

The girls' table had a covering the colour of cheap red wine. When Emily asked for a refill, the waiter with the boyish haircut sniffed her glass and said, "Merlot?"

"What about him?" she asked Hayley as he moved off.

"No way. Never a waiter. They flirt with everybody." The way she said it made Emily want to give the waiter back his smile.

After the set they followed Hayley's plan. They stood outside on the front steps of Hugh's and waited for the band members to come out on their break. The lead singer had said they were from Port Perry, didn't know anyone. Hayley said it'd be easy: these guys weren't used to girls like them. Hayley stood with one foot on a step, higher than the other. It made her legs look longer. Hayley bummed a cigarette off the first one out, the one with red hair. Emily tilted her head back on the exhale to draw attention to her low-cut top.

"What's that strange instrument you're playing? We've been trying to figure it out all night," Hayley asked.

He told them the name. It sounded like *pheromone*. Turned out he moves the sound waves. Turned out he's one of eight people in North America who play it. Turned out Eric Clapton had one on stage but he just waved his hand in it to say, *Hey, isn't this cool.*

The second-cutest guy in the band came out, his goatee tapping the air like a tiny hammer as he skipped down the steps. Hayley bummed a cigarette from him. She leaned her shoulder against his velvet suit and asked him about all those egos in a group. She touched his arm and said, "C'mon, you can tell me. Is there one guy in the group that everyone bows to?"

"No, we all take turns choosing songs. The rule is that it has to have the word *silver* in it or it has to have been written by a blind man." He named some musicians Emily and Hayley hadn't heard of. "We only know Ray Charles." He made good eye contact with both of them when he introduced himself, and he told Hayley and Emily they had beautiful names.

"I named my son Emilio," he said. The word *son* a sinker on a fishing line. Hayley took her leg down from the step.

But he kept going. "Yeah, my girlfriend—" He looked at the street and pointed to the British Morris Minor pulling up to the curb, right on cue. Driver on the wrong side. "There she is now."

When she stepped out of the car, Emily could see that her hair and smile were a thing together. He introduced her. Her boy hips, the kind Emily was working towards. They readjusted the circle, but it was a lifeboat with Velvet-Suit Man and Wrong-Side-of-the-Car Girl wanting Emily and Hayley out of the dinghy. He was looking at her neck and saying, "I bought that for her."

Emily saw a huge silver heart locket, same as the one she had in grade three. "Were you blind at the time?" She had finally said something, thinking she was clever and funny.

The girlfriend put her fingers to the locket and said, "I like it," the word *like* sounding like a kiss.

Emily backed off, knowing it was a big band. There were still nine-elevenths left.

By the break before the last set, Hayley and Emily were worried their luck was running out. Clusters of smokers were milling about the front steps, and when the guy with the bowtie came out, Emily knew she had to choose. She bummed a cigarette off him. He had eyes that had spent their life trying not to be singled out by the teacher.

"You guys are from Port Perry, eh?" Emily said. "You have the best Goodwill store. I got two pair of shoes there once."

"Yeah, I get a lot of clothes there."

Emily thought the light was going on between them, when the tuba player with the sheriff's badge on his vest came and asked to speak to him "over there."

Hayley was strong enough to know it was not them. She told Emily, "These men are just not hungry enough."

3.

"Men want a trophy whether they admit it or not. Someone on their arm who makes them look good. Just like we do."

Hayley leaned back on the cushions as she spoke. Emily knew breasts like that appeared larger because of Hayley's flat tummy. They were at the newly renovated Drake Hotel on Queen West. It'd been a few months since their last excursion. Outside the snow came down in big chunks. Inside were the usual poseurs, just below the too-cool radar.

"We always see someone famous here."

"You mean the two times we've come?"

Emily's back was to the rest of the bar and she was staring at the wall behind Hayley. Plywood with black felt appliqué shapes. Symmetrical inkblots.

"Look, there's Italy." Hayley had turned to examine the wall.

"Where?"

"The boot, there."

"Near Baba Yaga," Emily said. "The old witch who lives in the woods. Look at her hooked nose and her finger going like this. You know, the witch Vasilisa has to visit in order to kill the nice girl. The one who tells everyone, 'Yeah, I'll be what you want me to be.'"

"Looks like she's picking her nose."

"Yeah. With Italy."

"Look, there's Shrek with boobs."

Beside them, a fireplace. The stockings were hung by the chimney with care, their pink and red fishnet stretched to the point of boredom, toes anchored with marbles.

"Remember that game with the red and blue and white spongy ball in the toe of your leotards?" said Emily.

"No."

"You'd stand against a wall and whack it from side to side. *Hello, hello, hello, sir, / Are you coming out, sir? / No, sir? Why, sir? / La-la-la-la-la, sir . . . One, sir, two, sir / Not enough for me, sir.*"

"You mean you'd hit yourself with the ball? What's the point of that?" Hayley asked.

"No, you'd hit the wall and lift your leg."

"I still don't get the point."

"It's something you do if you've got no one to play with. I always had bruises."

"So I had this nightmare," Hayley said. "I was at school. No one else was there. It was just Joe and me in the office and we were about to have sex in the principal's room and then my dad came in and I hid and he told Joe he was there to pick up his daughter. Joe tried to get rid of him. 'No,' he says. 'I'm sure Hayley would want a ride. I'll just wait.'

And he sits in the chair, winter parka puffing up around his neck, staring straight ahead. What is that? I mean, is it that I always let my parents' expectations stop me from doing what I really want in life?"

"Well, if you go for Jung's theory, each person in our dreams is part of our psyche. I'd say the parent in you is blocking you from having fun."

"Wow, you're good."

"Yeah," Emily said. "My girlfriends in high school used to ask my advice. Because they knew my older sister had tons of boyfriends, so she knew how to French kiss before anyone. I pretended to ask her, but it was me giving them advice. Me, the fat girl who sat in the corner at school dances. I cried my way through high school because the boys I liked never liked me."

"Are you serious? I can't imagine that." Hayley had only known Emily as she was now. In that body.

"Yeah, I have this fantasy that one day those high school boys are all going to want me. Take this bar — I'll come in here and they'll all approach me and I'll crush each one like baubles on a candy necklace. It's like I'm suddenly okay to them because I got a waist and grew my hair long. They see me now, y'know?"

"So how did you give such good advice if you never had a boyfriend in school?"

"I watched from the sidelines. From the dark corners of the dances. Studied them all. The fat girl is the lowest a man can pick."

"If men are truly like that, why do we want them?" A guy with a furry black pimp hat walked by.

"He looks like the guy from Crash Test Dummies,"

Emily said. She turned to look where Hayley was staring. A group of men in their late fifties beginning to gather around a low coffee table behind Emily.

"What would so many old men—" Hayley began.

"Shhhh."

"—be doing out without their women? Do you think they wear suits during the day? Look at them, they're all smart-casual. I think they're from out of town. Movie producers. Okay, you have two minutes to guess what they are."

"I heard them say they meet every year. Let me listen for a bit." Emily leaned back in the chair.

"No, you have to guess now."

"I think they're old hockey players."

"I think they all went to high school together. And they've met every year since. Okay, now you have to ask them."

"I knew that was coming," Emily groaned. Hayley was heavily into the red wine. She didn't know white had fewer calories. After three glasses, the dares always began.

"You have to ask the cute one with glasses, but wait until I have a cigarette. There's a smoking room upstairs. We can take turns so we can keep this table. This is a prime table."

Hayley disappeared up the stairs. Emily scanned the Rorschach wall and found a komodo dragon.

She kept turning around to get a better look at the table of old men. The one in the red sweatshirt made eye contact every time. He was the one who made her discount the movie producer theory. Something about his haircut said suburbs.

The waitress had no hips and her stomach was a tiny inner tube encircling the top of her jeans. "What is edamame?"

Emily asked, pointing to the bar menu.

"Soya beans with sea salt and lime. They're great. I eat them all the time instead of chips," she said.

They came and, yeah, they were an eating-disordered dream. Like fat snow peas, you have to pop each pod with your mouth. Burning calories just to do that.

Emily's eyes followed the waiter with the ponytail around the room. She found a duck on the Rorschach wall. Her Ken doll used to have stick-on felt moustaches — a Fu Manchu, a handlebar, and the beard-moustache combo. She found them on the wall. A Kazakhstan video was projected on the stone over the fireplace. The landscape reminded Emily of some barren place where men riding horses look for a fight. The empty green edamame skins lay defeated on a napkin on the table. A few left floating in the bowl in a shallow brown pool of sea salt.

Emily looked up and there was Hayley coming towards her, swinging her hips and smiling, her drink out like a left-turn signal as it passed over the heads of seated loungers.

She had someone with her. He wore an Icelandic sweater. It bulked out like a boat as he sat down with Hayley.

"He's from Montreal," Hayley explained. He smiled like a sheep. "He came here alone. And guess how old he is." Like a Jewish matchmaker, except it was obvious he'd followed her to their table.

"Twenty-six," Emily said.

"How did you know? Wow, you're good." Hayley said.

"I just need to get a drink," he said, and slid a hand along Hayley's arm on the way to the bar.

"I'm sorry," Hayley said. "How are we going to get rid of him?"

He came back, nodding and smiling. "I'm Tom." His face was calm, but next to the Icelandic neckline she sensed a bleak landscape.

He smiled right into Emily. Which she was shocked at, then she remembered her new body. She always went through the same surprise.

"He went to school for cartography, then switched to English."

He did a smile with his head down, a cat giving one good lick to its paw. "Actually I learned how to design GIS systems. Do you know what those are?" Emily kept her focus on him, trying to block out Hayley's swallowed giggles. "They hold the complete information on a site. Take this place, the Drake, for instance. You could call up the heating system, the plumbing system, and how many times it's been changed over the years. The structure of the beams, the sewage system beneath. You can see everything at once."

"An archaeological history," Emily said.

"Uh, yeah. Wow. Yeah." He was really looking at her now. "What do you do?"

"I'm a teacher. Kindergarten," Emily lied. He told her about his kindergarten teacher and how she wanted him to sit on her lap and he didn't want to.

"Good call," Emily said. She could see his mind searching for the next topic.

"Have you heard of James Joyce? You should read *Ulysses*. You really should." Emily knew that was a book you had to read in university. She realized Tom was fresh from his English courses. This guy hadn't graduated to the real world yet.

He squeezed the edamame skins, looking for uneaten beans. Then started spinning imaginary phonograph records in the air like the DJ in the corner of the lounge. The girls desperately tried not to look at him. They talked about knitting. Emily told them about the Icelandic sweater she had knit for three solid weeks. On those circular needles you can never tell how far you've come, and by the time she looked up it was a sweater dress, the arms way past her hips. She didn't say it was because she'd mistakenly made it for her fat self. She had to cut a foot off the bottom and pick up the stitches to finish it off. The arms ended up way too short.

Tom lifted the white bowl and drank the edamame backwash. "I knitted a scarf once."

They stood up and put on their coats. Two people vultured into their seats. Tom stood.

"He comes with the table," Emily told the new people. She shook Tom's hand. His eyes still looked at her like they had a chance.

They left him and walked past the table of old men. Emily put her hand on one large leather shoulder. "What do you guys do, anyway? We're taking bets."

"Ex-cops."

"We both lost the bet, then." Emily said.

"I'm Frank." The red-sweatshirt man reached out his hand. Then he fumbled with his digital camera, held it at arm's length, and took a picture of Emily leaning over his shoulder.

"We meet every month. Next time you should come. Let me give you my card," Frank said, shuffling through a pocketful of other people's business cards. "Why can I never find a card when I meet a pretty girl?" He wrote his cell number, his home number, his email address, and *Xmas 2005* on the back of a card that said DON GIBBONS I.T. SUPPORT.

"We meet at Billy Bob's in the west end. We only ended up here because Billy Bob's is closed." She stuck out her ass and slid the card into the back pocket of her jeans, the way confident girls do.

Outside the Drake, Hayley and Emily stood recounting the story of Tom as if it had happened long ago. Tom parasiting himself. His hand snaking down their backs when he went to the washroom or to get another drink.

"I think he was brave," Emily said. "Look." She pointed up at the full moon.

"I hate the way you can never see stars in the city," Hayley said.

"I read somewhere that to see a star at its brightest, you have to look slightly off centre. It's the way the eye is designed. To see the star clearly, you don't look directly at it," Emily said.

"Like Tom's DJ spinning technique. Or when he drank from the bowl! Ohmygod, look away, look away!" Hayley laughed. "All in all, it was a successful night. Some men. Some fun."

"I've been thinking of reading *Ulysses*. Tom said I should."

"No one reads *Ulysses*."

"Wouldn't it be cool if you could design GIS systems for stars?" Emily said. "So someone could look at that star and see the earth, see Toronto, the Drake Hotel and us standing out here in the cold? If they could see right past our skin and our fat and our bones, right into our hearts? If they could tell everything about us?"

"Yeah, right down to the red lace underwear I spent a fortune on and never get to use," said Hayley.

"You know, you don't have to wait until next year to phone," someone yelled.

Emily turned. Frank had come out on the front steps for a smoke. He stared at the two of them linking arms as they made their way to the bus stop.

4.

Emily was biking in High Park and she heard some tinny music, sporadic drums. She rode until she came upon a crowd watching long-sleeved dancers lifting their knees as if demonstrating slow-motion soccer moves. A woman jogger had stopped beside her. "It's a Tibetan picnic. I heard it's the Dalai Lama's birthday."

Emily stayed for the singing. Someone passed a bag of white powder and she took a pinch and stood in a circle, raising her arm twice with the others before she threw the powder into the air along with them. Her dust landed on the Tibetan man in front of her. Four white spots in his black hair.

He said his name was Tashi. He invited her to sit with his family on a blanket. Offered her some dumplings and a boiled egg. He told her how he had to leave Tibet when he was nine. When he smiled, Emily watched his cheeks go up in points like a *commedia dell'arte* mask. One of his eyebrows a leathery fold of skin. He told her a long story that ended in Toronto, with him working in a belt factory.

He said, "Anything negative is small when you've been

through the big stuff." When her eyes wandered to take in the sights — the children playing badminton, families sitting on blankets under the trees, teenage boys cycling around selling DVDs of Tibetan dancing — Tashi touched her arm to bring her back. He said, "This is it," and he held his arms up to the picnic, and she knew to stay looking into his eyes, into all that pleasure.

Emily drank a Tibetan drink that looked just like lemonade, and afterwards she learned the names of all the people on the blanket. Then she excused herself. Tashi shook her hand like he meant it.

Back in her apartment, she sat on the couch. Looking out over the treetops. Listening to all the sounds from the street. Talk from the cafés. Sirens on Bathurst. Car doors slamming in the church parking lot. Kids laughing from fenced-in backyards. And somewhere a cat crying louder and louder, begging to be heard. *All those people*, Emily thought, *not one of them knowing where the sound's coming from.*

THE TREE MAN

I met the Tree Man at a party in Sydney — his long, curly hair, worn checkered shirt, thick leather vest. I liked his face, its many lines to read. We were drunk. We kissed and danced and when I asked him at the end of the night to call me, he gave me his tree-care pamphlet. A surgeon, specializing in thinning, reshaping, formative pruning. GIVE YOUR SAPLINGS A HEAD START FOR THE FUTURE. AVAILABLE 24 HOURS.

Our first date was sober. He picked me up in the long-bed truck, foliage, shrubs, hardwood piled high in the back. I spoke of trees metaphorically. The symbiosis of woodlands. The strange fig parasite killing its host. The discovery of skewed rings in a trunk that's spent its life fighting the wind. And although he had a genuine love of nature, he failed the test. Said he didn't write poetry but there was "definitely no shortage of concept, man," a line I jotted down in my mind.

In his warehouse apartment at Circular Quay he chopped some wood, turned out the lights, lit a huge fire, and switched the upstairs stereo on, soft jazz settling down on two armchairs by the fire. It was right out of a magazine. As I was about to give in to the temptation to ask if I could take a photo, he jumped up, grinning. Hooked himself into a tree harness as if it were a diaper, climbed a rope fixed to the ceiling, and abseiled from his upper loft bedroom back down to the living room, where I stood speechless. No one had ever rappelled for me before.

So we went to bed. His lips were dry and his hands scratched and coarse. He put his arm around my shoulder as if he'd just read the manual. *Place hand here.* He stripped down to his boxers, even slipped them off, then thought better of it when he saw me not removing anything. He climbed under a million blankets and pillows, pulling me into him. His arms and thighs wrapped around me as if braced for a fall. My face trapped in his armpit, the smell of wood and sweat. I kept pushing the covers back to get air and he kept rewrapping me. His gangly limbs clutching the soft sanctuary. *Death by smothering*, I thought, feigning sleep.

In the morning I woke to stiff kisses, hands on my breasts, and the line "I wish you'd lose some layers, 'cause I'm feeling really randy." Where was the poetry, the words painstakingly carved into chunks of wood by the fireplace while I slept?

He drove me home in the truck after a quick stop at the dump. Standing in my heels and long black dress, I watched the Tree Man toss his collection. Branches, stumps, deadwood flying from the back of the truck. In this act of removal, his body finally and absolutely alive.

LEVITATE

I lay like a corpse on the orange and brown rug in Cathy Bagg's basement. Tina, Brenda, and Cathy placed their hands under my back and hips. The spirits would take care of my feet and head, Cathy said. She turned out the lights over the simulated wood bar. Only the glimmer of upside-down wineglasses, their stems caught in the rack. Bats congregating for the show. Cathy read the chant from a book of spells she'd found at the public library.

Cathy's most recent phases of interest: cooking, poetry, and do-it-yourself dollhouses, all supported by the librarian and carried out by us. We made double-decker melted cheese and pickle sandwiches, recited Chief Dan George poems on the picnic table in her backyard, collected empty spools to convert into Barbie coffee tables. Whatever Cathy wanted.

I made my belly and limbs tight and long as an ironing board, praying to some god in the dark to make me rise above the shag carpet. I felt the warmth beneath Cathy's hands, spread wide like spatulas. Cathy leaning in, spilling words of incantation over my summer dress. Cotton, the lightest one in my closet. No underwear, just to aid the cause.

Tina opposite Cathy for "brown-eyed symmetry," like in *Math Puzzlers for Kids*. The two of them moved in unison. Under my hips was Brenda with the shuffling hands. Whenever Cathy said to be still, she shifted. I discounted her immediately. The spirits would interpret her as ambivalent. (Brenda soon after became ostracized from our group for wearing pants that were too short.)

It was Cathy I was depending on, and Tina, because Cathy believed in her. It was Cathy's words I drew into my veins like ginger ale sucked through crazy straws. I let them travel through me, knowing, absolutely, that I would rise.

I held Cathy and Tina as strongly as they held me.

The day the three of us were to go swimming in Cathy's pool, I cycled over in the hot, hot sun, banged on all the doors and the backyard gate, heard giggles but no answer. Rode all the way home and arrived as the phone rang. Could I come back over? They were only kidding. I said no. And let go the phone the way you'd let go a rope you thought was keeping you afloat. I didn't speak to them. At school I ate my lunch at their table, and when they asked me a question, I pretended I hadn't heard. Our lockers were side by side but I used my locker door like a shade to block out their faces. And when Cathy cried in remorse and her mother called my mother, I used her begging forgiveness to make me rise, inches above that floor.

HOW FAST THINGS GO

HUCK

So Prinkie comes into the backyard with his look-at-me walk, cigarette between his lips hanging on for dear life. He says to me What you been doing Huck? Something like that. He flips his hair back with two broken fingers that don't bend anymore, the same ones he uses to roll his joints. I give him another beer. He says it's warm, tilts it back so his neck is a long slow chug, Adam's apple jumping up. Margaret in the lawn chair, legs open. She's still in high school, cute, his usual type. He's sitting on the end, turned around so he can look at her crotch. Keeps grinning. The drink getting to his brain, blocking out the rest of us. He finishes off the beer, passes it to me, and I put it on the grass.

Then it gets strange. He starts saying his old man got kicked out of the Rex Hotel for who-knows-what, he's probably sleeping on some Queen Street subway grate. Then he's complaining about his mom and how she's got that disease, shakes every time she reaches for a coffee. How she spends a lot of time sitting on her hands. He makes some crack about her and the old man in the dark. So I make a joke, can't remember now, something about vibrating fingers. He's picking at the threads of the lawn chair then. Looking straight at me. I start to get worried, his eyes angry, stuck on me. Margaret's tense, cause she leans forward, puts her hand on his shoulder. Let's go inside, she says, but he isn't listening. His eyes are stuck on me. Says what do you mean by that? Nothing man, I say.

MARGARET

Prinkie's drunk when I get there, just like the first time he asked me out. I skipped school to be with him and all he wants is ten dollars for beer. He's pissed off when I just show him my bus fare. He calls his mom at the bank like he's a kid who lost his allowance, even though he's almost twenty. Funny part is she says yes. So we head over to the mall with his brother Tad. Laughing, joking. Prinkie showing off how good he can be to a girl, twirling a cigarette with his stiff fingers before he lights it for me. But something goes wrong when I say I need to buy towels for my cousin's wedding. I don't know what colour to get, and every store I go into, I touch the brown ones, then the pink ones, asking him what do you think? Prinkie doesn't like that. He pushes me in front of everyone, shoppers not caring. I'm thinking someone might see my scared face, my eyes filling up. But I know if I cry I'll just get it later. He pushes me again so I say forget the towels. Jesus, can't you decide about anything? he says. Maybe he's right.

The first time he hit me we were in his room. His mother never comes in when the door's closed. We were playing a game of caps, cross-legged on the floor. Prinkie in his cut-off jean shorts, no underwear. His penis peeking out the side. He aimed his caps at my breasts, giggling at every hit. We drank all afternoon till he passed out on the floor mattress and I snuggled up under his arm. I heard his mom go out around dinnertime and I just let it get dark in the room except for the TV.

He woke up later like he'd had a bad dream, started thumbing through his 45s in boxes on the floor, all alphabetical by artist. He's the guy you say a song title to and he can tell you the B side, the year, the record label. I think his place in the universe is a record store, helping people who come in humming a tune they don't know the name of. He started yelling because he couldn't find the Moody Blues' "Nights in White Satin." It was under N, so he knew Tad had been going through his collection. I told him it didn't matter but he got himself into a rage. I touched his arm and he threw me off, pushed me against the wall. He slammed the lid of the stereo so it broke and then he was almost crying, looking at the crack. He picked the whole thing up, smacked it on the floor. Opened the window and whipped it into the alley between the houses. It landed on the garbage hutch I climb in and out on so his mother doesn't know I spend the night. Then he started crying, said he was sorry for hurting me, that he doesn't want to be like his dad. He promised me it'll never happen again.

We're crossing the street on the way back from the mall when a little Honda Civic almost runs Tad down. He's walking slow with the two-four on his shoulder. The driver says get the fuck off the road and get a job. My big man Prinkie doesn't like this so he runs after the car to make it stop. And it does. Prinkie starts mouthing off to the guy through the open window. The driver says go home but Prinkie's going to get a fight today no matter what. This seven-foot guy gets out, Prinkie only coming to here on his chest. One tap on Prinkie's shoulder and *boom*, he's down, it's all over. Tad laughing and me starting the walk back. Prinkie taking the hurt in. I can tell he's building up to something.

At the house Prinkie gets on Huck's case for making some joke about his mother. He stands up, says come on Huck, come on. Huck stands up with his beer in his hand and says we've been friends since grade school, man. He looks hurt. No anger, just hurt. He sets the beer down, waves his hand at him as he walks away — he's giving him that. I'm shocked Huck cares, that someone else cares about Prinkie.

HUCK

So then Prinkie jumps me. Surprises me, takes me to the ground. What the hell's wrong with you? I push him off me. We're friends I keep saying. He takes a swing at my face but the booze makes him miss. Then I catch a punch with my belly. I push my fist straight into his mouth. His lip catches on his bottom teeth and I feel the skin of his cheek fold, something hard poking through. He lifts his hand to his face. Looks down at the blood. And I'm halfway down the street before he realizes he's got a hole in his cheek.

He comes tearing after me. And I stop like a wall waiting to meet him. All control gone out of his face now. He scares me. Goes to put his full weight into me but I move a little to the side. His balance is off, all I have to do is push him. He lands on the sidewalk. I know it's all out of him so I walk away quietly and leave him to crawl back to Margaret.

MARGARET

Huck's a good guy, walking away, but Prinkie takes off after him. A few of the guys come into the backyard saying they're fighting. I have a couple of bucks in my hand and some change from the beer so I leave it on the picnic table and run towards the road. I want to see them fight but then again I don't, so I turn around at the side of the house and walk back. Of course the money's gone. Where's my money? Tad pulls out the bills from his pocket, keeping the change.

That night, Huck long gone, some guy named Dog comes with some smoke and we pass it around Tad's room in the basement. Tad says Dog did it with his cocker spaniel, more than once. Did he get caught or just tell someone? Either way, I keep looking at him to see if it's true. I sit on the black couch, the front seat of Tad's old car, foam poking through, Prinkie beside me smiling, laughing. Everything calm now. Thick smell wrapped around me, safe till the next time. The hole in Prinkie's face like a slit. He keeps pinching it open, letting the smoke creep out for entertainment.

I go upstairs to the can. Walk past Prinkie's room with
the holes in the wall. He says that was the only time he was
in jail, for vandalism. He says he got off, someone must
have sucked off the judge because he was looking at three
months. The closet in the corner I never open since he told
me about the glue sniffing and the sex assault charge. He
says his fourteen-year-old cousin asked him to fuck her with
a hot dog. I used to believe everything he told me, up until
we went skating.

For months I told him I'd teach him. I have all my figure-
skating badges, I'm even an amateur coach at the arena.
Okay but go easy on me he said, I just wanna learn those
crossover moves like in the NHL. We headed to Scarborough
Town Centre in my dad's blue Pinto with the white racing
stripe, only this time we didn't buy a dime bag from Dog
and smoke behind the Staff Only doors.

We parked in the lot. Prinkie saw a purse on the front
seat of the car next to us. He circled the car, looking at the
locks. The back door was open. I looked around and there
was no one except lots of bushes that someone could come
through any second. He was itching, saying I'll be quick. I
screamed no and started walking, the guards on my blades
hitting my shins. He followed but his face was making plans.

He laced up slow, stepped on the ice, his ankles kissing
each other like a five-year-old's. I skated backwards, held
his hands in my amateur coach way. Then on the corner
he started crossovers, then T-blading into backward
crossovers, whipping laps, stopping sideways like a Maple
Leaf, spraying my tight jeans.

So I'm thinking he probably slept with Aggie, that girl
he lived with before he had to move back in with his mom.

That he wasn't a virgin when he met me, like he says.

I go upstairs to check my mascara cause maybe Huck'll come back later with some let's-be-friends-again pot. The door to the can's open. Prinkie's mother Joan is in there. She jumps when she sees me, like she always jumps when anyone comes into a room. The wallpaper's dirty pink but you can tell it used to be rose, and the green spotted border wraps around the bathroom like it's a present. The light above the mirror is two glass flowers, the stems bent as if a storm just hit. She's got my black liquid eyeliner in her shaky hand. Can you show me? she says. I draw it along the edge of her lashes.

I can't wear this anymore she says. I watch it going on silver, then in milliseconds it's gone. She looks at me all sad, like the brush only works for sixteen-year-olds, like there's lots she can't have, and cat eyes are just one more thing.

HUCK

It's his mother I feel sorry for. Look at who she's got — Prinkie and Tad. And Elaine, Prinkie's sister, is sure something. Always drinking at the Scott Tavern till someone phones her husband to come get her fat ass off the bar stool. She married him cause nobody drives a baby blue Cadillac unless they're money. Once they got hitched he sold it, then where were they?

I'm in the kitchen with Tad. Prinkie calls, he's on his way back from the courthouse. He's gone with his mom and Elaine's husband to prove to the judge a girl with a family wouldn't launder money. I don't know the details except I know Elaine did it. I guess things didn't go so good, cause Joan comes in hyperventilating, her skin all grey. She's rushing around the kitchen, putting things like reading glasses and cat food in a bag, saying you better get out of here, the judge said Elaine's a liar and Prinkie threw a fit in the cloakroom, he's on his way from the courthouse.

I laugh cause the last time he threw a fit we were both couriering for one of those big downtown banks. I got him the job, picking up envelopes and packages, all he needed was a cheap briefcase from Walmart. We'd duck into the washroom at First Canadian Place and see what he was carrying, smoke a doobie, then take the long route. First Christmas party he gets hammered. Comes home pockets full, five colours of Post-Its, a whack of highlighters and a long-arm stapler. Can't remember a thing, thinks he trashed the stockroom. He doesn't come in the next day and they call, where the hell are you? Like nothing ever happened. He thinks Eightball covered for him, the guy who sells uppers out of an Honest Ed's bag. He has one of those black balls on his desk, the fortune-telling ones, turn it over — yes, no, maybe. A week later they handcuff Eightball right in the middle of the office and he hands Prinkie his 8-Ball on the way out. Prinkie takes it as luck, but he gets fired right after anyway.

When he lost that job he was living at the shelter. He broke into his mom's house, punched her walls. She had the whole place fixed up except his room. You can come back and stay as long as you behave, she said. She left the holes to remind him to be someone else.

MARGARET

So she's sad about the eyeliner, says she's never been in love.

Not ever?

No.

Not even with Prinkie's dad?

No. Her eye twitching. I can see her ducking a punch.

What about Mr. Gray?

She calls him Mr. Gray even though they've been snuggling on the couch for more than three months, TV blaring.

Mr. Gray? She laughs. He's just a friend.

I don't think I would have sex with someone I called Mr. Gray. I think I'll just give up when my eyeliner stops sticking and I'm looking ahead, seeing no love in sight.

So I buy brown towels for the wedding, sign *Love from Prinkie and Margaret*, putting his name first so they'll think he put some money in. Prinkie's allowed to come as kind of a "gesture" on my parents' part. They blame him for my forty-eight percent in history. My mother didn't find out right away. She phoned the school, where's Margaret's report? It was under my bed with a big blob of white-out over the twenty in the Classes Missed column. History's when I met Prinkie at the mall. I botched the job. I wrote 2 overtop and the black marker kind of wound its way over the hardened whitener like an ant crawling over a bump in the sidewalk. They mailed her the report. She said you're skipping school to smoke drugs, you're probably pregnant. I screamed you won't even give him a chance.

Of course they forgave me later. Everything's forgiven when you're a girl with a black eye.

HUCK

It's in Kincardine, Margaret's cousin's wedding. I went to school with her. She's serious and smart like Margaret but without the cute wiggle. Margaret's parents let Prinkie come to the wedding even though it means paying for his motel room a couple of nights.

I think somewhere deep down Margaret knows it's the only way out. Like Prinkie won't be able to kiss their asses for longer than a day. He tries though. He even dances with Margaret's mom. A waltz. He's laughing too loud. Trying so hard to hold her right. I know those eyes — the open bar's too much for him. A real family's too much.

Her uncle drives us back to the motel, Margaret on Prinkie's lap beside me. He's whispering who's the guy you danced with? I don't care if he's your first cousin, something like that. It doesn't matter what she says. If she's smart she'll ask her uncle to take her back to her parents' hotel. But like I said, I guess she knows this is it. She has her uncle drop us at the room me and Prinkie are sharing. They go in and I sit outside on the curb, smoking a joint. They're not loud but it's pretty quiet in small towns so I can't help hearing. And the door's open.

I think it goes just the way she figured, except for the black eye. Prinkie yells you want to leave me? She says no, she loves him. Prinkie's crying about not being good enough, same as in grade school. Funny I'm not surprised he still does that. She tells him he is. Prinkie bangs something with his fists. She's begging now, saying how much she loves him. Margaret told me it's pretty much the same every time, he hits her somewhere no one can tell. So I'm picturing

Batman and Robin whacks to the head, punches to the stomach, kicks to the thighs. I get up and open the door wider. Margaret's lying on the bed holding her face. I can see the thought right there: *He punched someplace they'll notice.* He hit me she says. But it sounds like *finally.* She runs out to the sidewalk.

Then Prinkie's coming out of the motel, sorry sorry sorry. I put my arm around Margaret. She's not crying or anything. We start walking fast like a couple real late getting somewhere. Prinkie tries to grab her, carry her back to the motel, but she starts swatting him and I've got her by the waist. A man's walking his dog on the sidewalk, not saying anything. Then Prinkie gives up and turns back. Margaret and me walk to I don't know where, Margaret smiling like Dorothy going back to Kansas. A cop car pulls up beside us. I've got a young man here who says he's made an awful mistake. He drank a bit too much. My arm's still around her and I don't let go in case she might crawl in the back of that cop car and end the story same as always.

The next morning her father and me have eggs and fries at the diner, him talking big, he's going to fucking kill him. The motel room's empty, my clothes still there in a pile, my rolled-up socks on top like two eyeballs. At lunch Margaret sits on her aunt's couch. Everyone's there telling family stories, offering her egg salad sandwiches on Wonder Bread. No one says nothing to Margaret about the black eye. No one says nothing to her about Prinkie not being there. Her mother whispers to her ninety-year-old grandmother. Nan says loud What on earth did he do that for?

MARGARET

He hitchhiked back from Kincardine, I find out Monday from Huck. I say I don't care how he got home but I care all the way back to Toronto.

It's like I'm hooked on how fast things go from bad to good with Prinkie.

The first time I knew it could be that way was the whole thing with his dad and the money. His dad called, he was living on the streets, broke. His mom said fine but she wouldn't be there when he picked it up. She left the cash on the table and we were there when he knocked. Prinkie made a big show of looking, said he couldn't find it anywhere. He ended up punching his dad, calling him a liar, saying his dad stole the money. Imagine a homeless old guy and Prinkie all righteous, brawling on his mom's wall-to-wall burgundy carpet.

His dad left and Prinkie opened up the *Sunday Sun*, held up the $160 his dad never stole. I found it by accident he says to me, I was just checking out the Sunshine Girl. He says Huck used to poke her. I don't buy that. She doesn't look like Huck's type, her boobs hanging out, her lips all ready. He'd want someone who sticks with one guy.

After Kincardine I can hang up on Prinkie only so many times. It's the tears that do it. Before long I'm standing at his door. Prinkie grabbing his coat, jamming money in his Roadrunner jeans. Let's get Huck and celebrate he says, let's buy you something special. And I know we're heading to the beer store.

BELOW BELOW

They've given Naomi a room on the second floor. The view: smoothly paved university roads, sculpted islands of grass. *This place needs messing up*, she thinks. In the parking lot her Renault, the sloped back doors reminding her of the VW Beetle that time in Montreal. Big-top stuff, thirty white-faced clowns springing out to a drum roll . . . one more, ohhhh . . . the crowd pretending not to know the trick. *The necessity of an escape hatch*, Naomi thinks now, staring at the bunk beds.

She hauls her suitcase-on-wheels onto the lower bed, saving the upper for sleep, assuming there'll be no room-mate. She asked for a single room. She doesn't like the feel of someone above her. The suitcase springs open, a bouquet of blouses and skirts. Unlike the great moment of climax in her show with George, when both their suitcases sprung open to reveal nothing for their long journey.

Her first workshop since the divorce. It felt like she was gearing up for a performance. *Naomi Solo*, she could call it, a sequel to *Naomi and George*. One lost soul instead of two.

They'd had a fair run in small theatres across Canada; the reviews kept the money coming. Audiences weren't particularly cultured but they somehow seemed to feel the resonance with Beckett, even if they'd only skimmed *Waiting for Godot* in some humanities course years ago. *Maybe I'm fooling myself*, she thinks. *We were more like Laurel and Hardy. Or Abbot and Costello.*

Their show was dimly lit for the whole hour and a half. Next to Naomi, George looked like a Guinness Book of Records giant. When he angled his salt-and-pepper beard towards the overhead lights, it was clear he was the one to be counted on. Even with his fingers poking through the holes in his overcoat pockets, the toe of his left shoe separating from its sole. Naomi was his round, unsmiling companion with a worn suitcase, smaller than his, at her feet. The too-big grey overcoat, three round buttons hanging a little loose, making her look like a scorched snowman. They would both peer anxiously down the empty train track.

Brett said he might come visit the university midweek. It's taken three months of dating to successfully convince him she's the kind of confident woman who runs off to Buffalo to teach. She's just glad he wants to get into her pants and not her tax returns, seeing how he's a retired accountant. Except for the height, everything about him is anti-George. The pants never without a belt, the pause followed by the full sentence. Wouldn't even consider folding himself into a VW Bug. When she pictures him in clown nose, he's the whiteface Joey. The victim of a nattering fly while trying to read the paper in peace. Neither arriving nor leaving. The one willing to wait a long time at the bus stop. When she'd said, "I'm a clown," it was as if someone had held a buttercup under his shiny chin. She hadn't lit anyone up like that since George.

She takes out her pyjamas — George's old green tartan pair — lays them on the residence bed, spreads the arms out, and crosses one leg over the other at the knee, as if he's greeting her at the end of a hard day. She closes the suitcase. By her bedside, a large jar of butterscotch candies, cocoons past hatching. She hopes they will last the week. Hopes she has the stamina to deal with this group each day, all day.

"Instructor Naomi Michaeloff trained in the Lecoq movement method and has toured with Cirque du Soleil. No previous theatre experience necessary." She'd purposely left the description terse, ambiguous. Lecoq, of course, would have had a fit at seeing her introduce novices to such sophisticated physical theatre games, but Lecoq was very dead. She hadn't attended the funeral in '99 for fear of running into George and her other classmates. She hadn't wanted them to see how wide she'd grown. And Paris was too far, the flight too long to sit still. She pictured Lecoq's open coffin, the smirk on his mouth, her leaning in, holding out her hand, feeling for breath. His eyes popping open in the grandest entrance of all.

She'd been accepted by the school in Paris along with eighty-nine others from around the world. No one else from Bumfuck-Nowhere, Ontario. It was her ticket out, the biggest ticket of all. Classes were conducted in French; fortunately, Naomi's mother was French Canadian, so she knew enough to get by. The training was rigorous: movement analysis included acrobatics, juggling, stage combat. But she was fit and nimble. The improvisation part came easily to her. Lecoq had said, "*Vous êtes supérieure.*" The collaborations, on the other hand — themes such as shame, betrayal, love — were deeply frustrating and difficult.

Such as the piece in which she looked out a window and caught her love sailing away in a boat. Her two sidekicks, on either side of her like bookends, turned away from the portal, oblivious. She cried like a wounded dog, then twisted away from the view. Just as the two turned back to the window. Their timing needed to be impeccable, but no matter how much direction she gave them, the performance fell flat. She broke down, yelled at them like Lecoq.

Only thirty were selected for the second year of melodrama, buffoonery, tragedy, and *commedia dell'arte.* She dropped out midway. Lecoq had said, "*Vous êtes impossible,*" but Naomi knew she intimidated him. Even Lecoq, a master of stripping away ego, showed his in the end. George, on the other hand, had a way of letting the verbal assaults roll off, and he managed to graduate before they stole away to big-city Toronto. Their happy bohemian life, rooming with other artists, busking and touring southern Ontario in a dilapidated van. Any possibility of acting was worth following.

What she misses most is the post-production high. She remembers her first show, the after-party, reliving each moment of the play with her fellow actors, and then driving home alone. George had left earlier in a huff. The buzz of the night filled the car, but loneliness was there too, a feeling she would become familiar with over the years. She replayed the bits where she'd shone, brilliantly improvised scenes that would never be recorded or developed. Sucking the moments like hard candy. The fight she'd had with George completely forgotten. When the cop pulled her over, he put her in the back seat of the cruiser and asked if she'd had anything to drink. Asked her to blow into the little tube. "No," she told him. "I've been in a play."

Back at home, the I-signed-up-for-a-family whining from George continued as soon as she opened the door, as if the play had been intermission to the argument. He said pshaw to all the studies about smoking and infertility. Said it was her. But Naomi wasn't buying it. She told him even eighty-year-old beer drinkers think they're shooting superheroes.

‹ ‹ ‹

Naomi arrives early for the workshop. She looks around the big room, the blue carpeted floor, the blue carpeted walls. Appropriately padded. She sits in the only chair in the empty room and looks up to find herself perfectly framed in a long mirror at the far end. First glimpse when the curtain opens. Horrible.

One hand grips the chair as if it were an airplane seat mid-turbulence. The other lies on top of her belly, thumb compulsively circling the tips of her first two fingers, trying to find their snap. The line where her white blouse tucks into her black Lycra skirt is a road going over a hilltop. Her ankles crossed. Legs sausages trapped in caramel nylons, three shades darker than her skin. Her hair is boy-short but she's left tufts sticking straight out, like bangs that don't want to sit. That edge of lawn the mower always misses, the bits that require a weed whacker. Her mouth sucking butterscotch, her lips a nursing baby's. Her eyes squinty, their resting state. Like a judge listening to a case that tests the limits of the law.

The door opens. A pudgy woman enters, half Naomi's age.

"Miss . . . Mrs. Michaeloff?"

"*Bonjour*," Naomi says.

She walks towards the side of the room opposite Naomi, then sees the mirror and heads to stand near the window instead.

Another woman arrives, also in her twenties. Sits on the floor, fiddles with a notebook.

Next a few middle-aged women wander in. Naomi nods as if ticking off a list, and they move quickly across the room to the periphery, placing sweaters and notebooks on the few stacked chairs. A tall boy strolls in, face TV-commercial strong. He sticks out his hand.

"Tony."

"*Bonjour*, Tony. *Je suis Madame Michaeloff.*" Her hand goes out and she feels her eyes widen, a lizard catching light. The rest of her still, ankles never parting.

He stands near the centre of the room, does a few side twists and knee bends as if warming up for a Saturday run. Each time the door opens, everyone looks. A girl, not more than sixteen, long blond hair curtaining her face. Another young man, ridiculously skinny, sporting a brown felt porkpie hat. A few more ladies on the edge of menopause. All find a place in the room as if walking towards their X, then turn to scan each new entry the way you do in an elevator, deciding who to rely on if it jams, who'll be sacrificed in a rescue operation.

Naomi takes out a miniature tambourine and a tiny drumstick. *Thwack. Thwack.* They all stand frozen.

"*Bien!* Jacques a Dit! You all know the game? *Oui?*" Brandishing her best Parisian accent.

They look at one another.

"Simon Says! *Oui? Jacques a dit,* move like a taxi driver." *Thwack thwack thwack.*

They travel around the room, turn invisible steering wheels. The occasional horn.

"Like a bicycle now! Aha! Jacques did not say bicycle." Naomi's drumstick is in the air like a flag. Hands fall off handlebars.

She dislodges herself from the chair. Feels the fat of her belly shift, a life preserver around her hips. She smells her own breath — butterscotch — as she gently taps a woman's back-side with the drumstick. She hits the others the same way, except Tony. She stands on tippytoe, a teetering ballerina, to rap him on the head.

The door opens. An old woman's face on a girl's body.

"Is this Clowning Around?"

Naomi looks at the group, her face a question. They nod yes.

"*Jacques a dit,* on the bus. *Vite, vite, tout le monde!*"

The newcomer joins in as they herd quickly towards the centre of the blue carpet, to where Tony stands, tipping his invisible hat, taking tickets. They shuffle two by two, the accepted ringmaster beating her tambourine.

After Jacques a Dit, Naomi moves on to the schoolyard game of Grandma's Footsteps. They say they've never heard of it. She puts Tony at one end of the room and stands beside him. Her body automatically teeters on her small feet the way it did onstage next to George, whose legs were long as trees. She tucks her head into her shoulders, looks up to meet Tony's gaze, his big face shining down on her like George's.

When she grabs Tony to turn his back to the group lined up along the opposite wall, she feels the hardness of his upper arms beneath his shirt. Quickly instructs them in her strongest LeCoq voice "*Pointe fixe!*" every time he turns around.

"Oh, it's Red Light, Green Light," someone says, and Naomi pretends not to know this, being from Paris and all. She walks over to the sidelines. Tony exemplifies Grandma, ordering people back to the start when he catches one of them moving. The whole group begins to tighten, to freeze on a dime. The new Grandma will be the one to successfully reach Tony first.

"You Canadians, so polite! Of course, now we understand the game, who will cheat?"

Naomi steps from the sidelines and pretends she has been sent back by Grandma. As she passes one of the older women, a frozen marathoner, she gently nudges her so she loses her balance and has to return too.

They begin to act like children at recess. Self-consciousness dropping to the floor like a pair of oversized pants, the adrenalin palpable in their focus on Grandma. She watches Tony become full ringmaster, alternating quick turns with long, teasing stares. "I saw you breathe! To the wall!" He understands timing. She can't teach that.

Naomi is obvious in her favouritism but she doesn't care.

‹ ‹ ‹

On the second night Brett calls Naomi from the highway.

"Have you ever seen Niagara Falls at night?" he says.

So the romance continues, Naomi thinks.

She stands in the window until she sees the green MGB convertible, Brett's retirement present to himself. As it winds towards her along the empty road, she thinks of the board game Life, the tiny plastic car that travels along the squares, hoping to avoid tragedy. *Lose your first husband, miss a turn. Hit menopause, back to the beginning.* She can picture him precisely, snug in the tan leather seat like the blue peg she'd always place in the driver's seat the moment her pink pin landed on MARRIED, SKIP AHEAD TEN SPACES. The crease along his thighs where he ironed his jeans. His knees open as if he's kicked back in a lawn chair, wrist slung over the wheel, his usual calm.

But he circles the parking lot and heads out of sight. She remembers she mistakenly told him the Richmond Building instead of Spaulding. She calls him on his cell.

"I just watched you drive away."

There's silence, as if he's unsure of his next line.

They head to a lakefront park. Walk arm-in-arm along the pier. Without planning to, Naomi stops. "*Pointe fixe!*"

"What's that?"

"It means 'fixed point' in French. When you don't know what to do, do nothing. *Pointe fixe*, and something will come."

"Something?"

"Something. You know, something that will make the audience love you. Clowns just want love."

"Is that all?"

"No, not all. We're like hobos. We live on the edge of town and come in to hold up a mirror to society. *This is who you are.* Then we disappear again."

She's talking fast and *pointe fixe*-ing often. Once she trips on purpose, bumps into him, forcing him into the role of silent sidekick. It's cold on the dock, and there is a whiff of sewage with each gust of wind. St. Catharines, they decide. She hurries him back to the car. She asks him to put the top up to escape the foul smell.

"Be patient."

She feels scolded, holds her breath as he reverses out of the parking lot.

She focuses on the air on her face, racing towards the Falls, not a star in sight. There won't be another man like George, she tells herself. He understood the game, understood her.

She decides to cut down on the clown talk, the clown act. The famous light display is on. They pass huge spotlights, strong enough to reach across the chasm of water and hit the falls.

"A spilled rainbow," she says.

"That's a lot of energy used up just for a show," Brett says.

They drive beneath the beams, and although they are far above her, Naomi ducks.

‹ ‹ ‹

The fertility test had shown FSH eight, a fine number, considering she was forty-three. On her optimal days she'd

put on the nightie that showed everything. Not telling
George, because the whole schedule approach had been
having adverse effects.

The first pregnancy had quietly miscarried. The second
made it to the day the books said it was safe to tell. The
third tissue biopsy showed it was George's Y chromosome
putting a nail in it every time.

‹ ‹ ‹

Tony leaves midweek, before the class graduates to become
baby clowns. Says he has an audition for an aftershave
commercial. Naomi looks at who is left: a motley crew.
What's the point now that her favourite is gone? The
menopausal ladies are waiting to go home to their families,
tell a few stories, scrapbook their photos in albums. The
younger ones are tolerable, particularly Pudgy. She knows
when to hold her neutral mask.

"Expect a surprise on Thursday," Naomi tells them. She
gets to the room early, lays out three garbage bags worth of
Goodwill clothes at one end of the room, a giant rummage
sale. She watches each student open the door and spot the
clothes as if someone were shouting "Surprise!" She makes
them wait at the other side of the room. Gives each a clown
nose dangling on a white elastic thread. She pulls hers on
around the back of her head and lets the nose rest on her
forehead.

"You must always breathe the nose onto your face.
Premièrement, look at the horizon until you see yourself.
Then breathe in the energy from all four compass points."

She's using the Pochinko technique, but these amateurs

don't know any better. Naomi hasn't worn her nose in ages. She stands in the centre of the room and uses her hands to pull the air towards her.

"North of north, south of south, east of east, west of west," she chants, turning to the four corners.

"Above above," she says, her hands tugging on the air overhead.

"Below below," she says. Pulls as if lifting water from a well. She feels the familiar energy run through her arms and legs, travel to her belly, her lungs, her heart. Even though she hasn't performed in years, she feels her clown waiting.

"The nose, the world's smallest mask, can see in all directions," she says.

Naomi takes a deep breath and lifts the red nose from her forehead. The elastic tightens around the back of her hair. She brings it down snug onto her face and adjusts it so the thread cuts into her cheeks.

She moves towards the pile of clothes, tentatively reaches out for a vest, decides no. She holds a pair of baggy pants up to her waist, then tosses them. Tries on a pair of long red gloves, pulls them up past her elbows. Looks at the audience, shows them she's satisfied. Her fingers become beaks, two birds bowing to one another. After each movement Naomi makes eye contact with individual students. She is in full clown mode. Her ego purrs in her belly, about to leap and growl and overtake the room. Instead she stops, breathes off her nose, and lets it hang like a jewel at her throat.

"*C'est ça?* Do you know what to do? Let the pieces speak to you. Your baby clown is deciding what to wear."

She watches them breathe on their noses, sees them pause after the four compass turns, trying to remember *above above, below below*. They're using their minds, not the place of clown logic. All except Pudgy. She seems to move from her belly, having successfully turned off her thoughts. Naomi watches her discard several pieces before climbing into a full yellow jumpsuit. Probably a handmade Halloween costume, part of a grown-up Tweety Bird or a banana. Its shiny, puffy quality and the way it fits tightly across the plump girl's form make her look appropriately vulnerable. An absurd snowsuit. And then, intuitively, the girl ties up her short hair, attempting a minute ponytail on top of her head. *Perfect*, Naomi thinks. *An impotent antenna. Just what I would have done.*

"You," she says, pointing to the only male left in the class. "Lie down! *Tout le monde, vite*, circle him, tight."

The porkpie hat is still on the young man's head, supplemented by a too-small tartan vest, pants that reveal bare ankles. He curls up like a fetus inside the circle.

"*Tout le monde!*" Naomi says. "Let sounds come. Any sounds. Soft sounds. *Souvenez-vous*, this is birth. Soothing sounds, then let it crescendo. And you, Porkpie Boy, when you feel it coming, you are ready to come out of the womb. Jump up and say your name."

"Which name?"

"Your clown name. It will be on your lips. Let it come."

Each person is born that day, with names like Phleep, Boju, Pleu-leu. Most sound French. When it comes to the yellow jumpsuit's turn, the girl lies like an earlobe on the blue carpet, squirming with her eyes closed. The group coos and begins to sing what sounds like a lullaby. She rolls onto her back as if asking for a belly rub; the group hums "Rock-a-bye Baby" and the girl pitches back and forth. Then suddenly she pushes herself up to stand, eyes still closed, swaying on her two feet, slightly at first, then it grows, as if her feet are two ends of a seesaw, arms out. The group moving away from her just enough that her outstretched fingers can't touch them, an intimate game of Blind Man's Bluff.

Her body stops, her eyes open. She squeals her new name. "Michaeloff!"

After the sounds die down and she is no longer beaming at the new world, she looks over at Naomi. "Sorry. I can change it if you want."

"You stupid child. Did I ask for such stupid children?"

Naomi consciously wears her angry mask, the one that her face so often returns to these days. But she feels a little smile in her chest, under her left ribs, where she pictures her red nose living when not in use. Someone has fallen in love with her after all.

‹ ‹ ‹

The only reason she witnesses the early-morning escape is because she can't sleep. The anxiety of the final day, the inevitable letdown afterwards. Naomi has given Pudgy Michaeloff a short *commedia dell'arte* script to practise, pointing to the lines for Arlecchino. Most of the others are revising pieces, but she wants to see how Pudgy handles the new material. She is to play opposite Il Capitano, Arlecchino's boss, a braggart obsessed with power and sex. But Porkpie Boy is putting his suitcase in the trunk of his car. At first Naomi thinks he's just highly organized, must be leaving tonight right after the closing party. But then he gets into the car and drives away. Naomi's not bothered. Il Capitano would have fumbled the ball anyway.

Pudgy looks appropriately terrified when Naomi tells her.

"All clowns must leave the stage eventually," Naomi says. "They lose all that love, but that's not for you, is it? Today is yours."

The scene starts with Pudgy entering through the fire exit in her too-tight yellow jumpsuit. The class sits cross-legged along the periphery. Pudgy is looking above their heads, sauntering past them with her hands behind her back. Her face all dreamy, a man in love.

"*Arrêtez!* I don't believe you are in love. Try again."

Pudgy enters again. Looks up at the same clouds, breathes in the sun, skips a little, then settles centre stage.

"No, no, no. Again. More. Exaggerate ten times."

She enters as if drunk with love, stops to pick a flower, smells it with all her heart, hugs it to her chest.

"Do you not know love, girl?" Naomi says.

She stands fixed.

"What is love? No, don't look at me. The answer is not on my face. *Pointe fixe.* The answer is in your body."

She stands for so long Naomi can hear the class hold its breath, willing her to figure it out.

"For god's sake, girl. Get down on the ground and put your nose in the whole flowerbed. Sniff it like a dog in heat, roll around in it, dreaming of your love, Columbina. As if she is the flowers."

Pudgy rolls around the carpet, Naomi directing her, pushing her through the scene until she is cartwheeling across the field, enacting stolen kisses, hands roaming, fondling an imaginary lover, her whole body shuddering with expectation.

"Bravo," Naomi says. "No Capitano necessary, *oui?* Bravo."

Naomi feels so alive. As if she were Arlecchino, high off the ground, prancing, unable to land. One of the students shows digital photos she's taken of Naomi directing. She is impressed with the elasticity of her face. The way it conveys such opposites: grief, ecstasy. She still has it. Naomi pretends to watch the other performances, but she is replaying her finest moments. This is nothing like real life. If only George could see her now.

TO THINE OWN SELF

I looked up in time to see the shutter close. I couldn't see Ben, just his arm coming out from behind the wall, holding the camera up periscope-style. I'd assumed my usual position in the living room, corner of the couch, reading. The floor lamp like a too-heavy sunflower. Jane Austen trying to catch the light. Gaineil had brought it without a bulb when my brother asked her to move in. *My dowry*, she called it, along with an unopened tin of marjoram, brittle bay leaves, a tiny pillow of turmeric.

I knew I wasn't in the shot. Yet another photo of Gaineil. Her face, makeup-less, overexposed, at the other end of the couch. A woollen mermaid in the wheat-coloured afghan. Harpo, her dreadlocked poodle, camouflaged in the folds.

The Discovery Channel was on low. Two guys blowing things up, realizing their long-time dream: a beer keg in the campfire. Dowsing the logs with lighter fluid. Crouching behind a Plexiglas screen like X-ray technicians.

Ben came around the corner, fiddling with the camera.

"Look, gorgeous." He stood in front of her, showing her the tiny screen.

She said, "At least I've still got breasts."

He bent down to kiss her slowly. "You'll be sexy no matter what."

He went to sit on the loveseat, then jumped up, remembering that the yellow-daisied slipcover was held together with pins. He didn't want it coming apart because of him. Sewing: just one of the things Gaineil had put on hold.

She'd been shaving her left armpit, going in all directions to get the cross-hairs, when she found it. She'd hung the HOW TO EXAMINE YOURSELF card from the showerhead like a DO NOT DISTURB sign long before that. I think she figured hanging it would be enough.

A friend brought an amaryllis to the house when she heard the news. Gaineil placed it on the sideboard and we all waited for the tip of the green stalk to plump, then split. "That's disgusting," I said. From cock to cunt in a matter of days. The little marker in the soil showed a postage-stamp photo of a salmon-coloured flower.

"Jeez," she said. "Why salmon? If you're going to take the time to come out, at least wear a red dress."

Each time Ben watered it, he said he felt as if he were encouraging a tumour. But he said that only to me. Secrets in the house starting to accumulate about then.

"It was me that fixed her tire, you know," he told me.

"I know."

"What do you mean you know?"

"I saw you."

We were both working the day Gaineil first came into Bar Mercurio. At first I thought she was a boy. A Beatles knockoff in skin-tight mod jeans. Short black hair slicked flat. The Peter Pan chin. Her bomber jacket's puffy epaulettes. As she turned, two things said *girl*: a pink elastic O at the base of her skull hiding a ponytail, and her long eyelashes that signalled monarch migration with one flutter.

"Just a coffee," she said, showing me her hands, as if that were the price of an americano at the bar. "The chain came off my bike."

I gave her a napkin, but she only half wiped before gulping the steaming hot coffee. The white cup like an unearthed bone in her filthy fingers.

"I've got a flat too," she added. "It's never just one thing."

I watched Ben's bald head catching the light as he manoeuvred around tables in his usual unconscious dance. I love that about him. Born to wait, I always tell him. "Take a look in the mirror," he says back.

The tips like a drug, keeping us both from bigger dreams. Ben had left Mercurio twice, both times to follow a girl. First to Chicago for Laney's internship at the Art Institute. She was using her specialties, Dada and Surrealism, to work through sexual abuse by an uncle. Then to Flin Flon, Manitoba, a one-pub town where Ben served mostly beer at the Unwinder. Tina had landed a job in Government Mineral Resources, not far enough away from her incarcerated ex-boyfriend. Ben the consummate gentleman, the distressed-damsel magnet. I was glad he always came back to the bar.

The next time he left I hoped it would be for photography school.

We had left Gooderham, with its general store still selling those banned bug coils, right between the Toothy Critter fish lures and Kawartha Dairy milk. Ben came to Toronto a month before me. Neither of us wanting to watch our mom drink herself to death. We left that to Dad. We got an apartment just down the street, 144 steps from Mercurio, with a mini-mart and a laundromat along the way. It doesn't feel Big City because I never leave the 'hood.

My friends are the other wait staff. They're all on stopovers on the way to a career in film or theatre or art. "What's your medium?" Brian once asked. At the top of his résumé: Puck's understudy, Shakespeare in the Park.

"Actually, I take a small." He laughed, and it was enough to distract him from asking anything else.

A month working in Mercurio is like a year of watching *Coronation Street*. I can see the storylines coming: the hot new waitress, the young boys vying for her. Strong, silent Brian, the only bartender capable of landing her because he was once in a movie with Donald Sutherland. A jealous husband, a rumoured pregnancy. Then there are the subplots of the customers. The middle-aged men dripping with delusional hope, straightening their ties at the short-skirted twenty-somethings huddled in packs. Books written in back corners, job interviews conducted through a martini haze. Status established with an expensive wine.

I'm rarely asked for my story. I think it's because I keep the eye contact light. I stay on the periphery because, honestly, I don't have a story. When someone in Gooderham asked what I wanted to be, I always said, "Outta here."

That day, when Ben caught sight of Gaineil, he swung
behind the bar and grabbed the Coke gun. She hadn't
removed the canvas bag from her back. The ultimate bike
courier, dodge and weave. I could tell he was nervous
because he stared at the froth awhile before giving her that
smile that gets the big gratuities. I knew no one had ordered
a Coke. That's how it was right from the beginning. Gaineil
was a high-pitched dog whistle across a windy park.

"Bike trouble, eh?" he said.

"Yeah, I hit a patch of ice. I was trying to avoid this pile
of snow near the light, and out of nowhere I was sliding."
Her open palm cut the air.

Ben was staring at her wrist the way you might check a
waif for scars.

"I'm just going to leave it chained out front. I've got to
get this package downtown before noon."

Ben heard his name and disappeared into the kitchen.
She handed me her money. I eyed her chunky silver ring.

"What does it say?"

"To thine own self."

"What?"

"*Be true* didn't fit. I made it at a jewellery shop on College."

"Wow. Can I see it?"

She handed it to me and I felt the letters. Rubbed where
the S was disappearing.

"I didn't carve it deep enough."

"Are you an actor or something?"

"No. It's a promise ring."

I laughed but she didn't laugh back.

The minute surgery was scheduled, Gaineil went into chronic PMS. The kind women use in defence trials. She'd pace around the house. Scream without warning: *What's this doing here? Who put this here?* Picking up a magazine, a set of keys, a pack of cigarettes. Any book I was reading, she'd whip out the bookmark and put it back on the bookshelf.

The worst was the fridge. She'd stick her head in, arms flying up, surrendering Baggies with half-eaten cheeses. Tupperware with carrots swimming in cabbage. Styrofoam trays with hard-edged prosciutto. She'd stuff the garbage and wet-waste bins so full their mouths couldn't close, and leave them like that until one of us did something about it. She'd get calm only when all the sauces and condiments were jammed into the corner of the shelf in a bomb-shelter huddle. I'd open the door, whisper to the ketchup, "It's safe to come out. She's gone."

She'd had a lump removed a few years before. Benign lipoma, they called it. A congealed ball of fat. Almost everyone has one somewhere in their body. She said the doctor held it up for her to see, hanging from his long-armed tweezers. It was a glowing orange sac, "like a reluctant sunset," she said.

Gaineil stopped going to work. Ordered DVDs off the Internet. Only went out when she saw the postal van pulling up in front of the house. She met the postie on the steps, took the brown box from his hand as though it were a rainforest remedy packed in dry ice. The titles: *Into Thin Air: Death on Everest*, *Race to Dakar*, *The Vendée Globe: Disaster Around Cape Horn*.

Once I came home from the bar at midnight; Ben had to stay till closing. Gaineil was asleep on the couch, fortressed with cushions. Harpo curled up into her stomach, oblivious to the dogs barking on the screen, straining in their pink harnesses, waiting for the command. Their musher wore a pink fur coat, long and full like a swing dress. A Finnish doll on her way to the dance hall.

I looked at the box: *Iditarod: The Great Sled Race.* The narration competing with sentimental music.

"The Rainy Pass. The most difficult part for DeeDee Jonrowe, who had to scratch here last year on the 200-foot hill down into Dalzell Gorge. Lots of glare ice and open water. She broke her pinkie. Her bones were still weak from the chemo."

I stood watching DeeDee and her dogs tear past the WATCH YOUR ASS sign. Her hands anchored on the handlebar, her legs sometimes clotheslining out as the dogs tore over pits and bumps in the trail.

"DeeDee's coming back from a double mastectomy in 2003. Three weeks after chemo, she placed 18th. She has the fastest time of any woman in the history of the race."

The DVD cut to a few other mushers in top spots, then back to DeeDee in a midnight pit stop in Rohn. The camera lit her in a halo as she moved to check the harnesses. She scolded a dog that was nipping at its partner. The dogs and DeeDee had white pupils, like in a zombie movie where only the viewer can see the truth.

She stood on the sled, both hands on the rail as if pushing a shopping cart. "Are you ready?" DeeDee said. Her singsong voice was unexpected. I looked at Gaineil and she was awake now. We watched all sixteen dogs instantly respond to the gentleness.

One day Ben asked me to cover his tables for the lunch hour. Gaineil had phoned. She was at the walk-in clinic.

"She's hemorrhaging," he said.

"What? Is she pregnant?" I said.

"No, no. I would have told you that."

He didn't return until after the dinner rush.

"She's fine," he said. "She quit the pill mid-cycle. Her doctor told her it would lower the risk of breast cancer. But then she read in some magazine that it actually accelerates it, especially if your mother had it. As soon as she saw that, she freaked out."

"So she's home? Does she need anything?"

"They just told her to go to bed with a box of tampons and watch soaps for the day. She looked so flushed and beautiful there in the waiting room."

I was struggling to take off Harpo's lead for the third time that day. Dog-walking had fallen to me. He stood on his hind legs, straining to get to Gaineil on the couch.

"I think Ben's going to propose," she said.

"What gave you that idea?"

"Has he said anything to you?"

"No, why?"

"I thought he'd've asked you to help pick out the ring."

"What ring?"

"I heard him on the phone with John saying, 'I can't talk.' There was a long pause and then he said, 'That's correct.' Like a game show host. Then, 'Oh, the damage is much worse. Visa called about unusual activity on my card.' I just hope he went with a square diamond. He probably hasn't even noticed I don't wear gold."

"Honestly, Gaineil, I wouldn't—"

"None of my rings has disappeared for sizing. If he asks you, they're in a drawstring Scrabble bag in my underwear drawer. The lapis lazuli is the only one that fits my ring finger."

Harpo got free, jumped up on the couch, licked Gaineil's face, and curled up with her. They say dogs instinctively know when someone's sick.

Even with Mercurio's mahogany wall panels, dark granite bar, and heavy marble floors and tabletops, it felt lighter being there.

"She thinks you're going to propose, Ben."

"Propose?"

"Do you think if I had Gaineil's long eyelashes someone would propose?" I widened my eyes like Sophia Loren and turned to pose in the mirror behind the bar. Ben looked at me.

"I didn't think she was remotely interested in marriage."

"She has cancer."

"What's that supposed to mean?"

"I think it's like being drunk. After a bender, what is it you always say? *I wasn't myself.* But what do I say? *Booze helps me be more myself.*"

The night before her surgery, Gaineil and I lined up six tequila shots each on the kitchen table. She didn't know if she'd be coming home with one breast or two.

"Do you ever wonder what they look like when you're on top? I mean, it can't be pretty," she said.

"I don't want to think about it. That's why I stay on the bottom."

"Yeah, but then they flatten out and slip down into your armpits."

We were on our fourth tequila. Gaineil lay on the floor on her back. "Like this. Okay, you can't tell. I'll have to take off my bra."

She struggled with the clasp under her top. Men are right. Bras are impossible. "My first boyfriend raped me, you know."

"What?"

"But it's not rape when you're at his place, in his bed."

"Did you tell anyone?"

"My best friend. She said it didn't sound like rape."

"Wow. Everyone knows that if you say rape, then it's rape. How could she not have believed you?"

Gaineil gave up fighting with her bra and lay flat on her back, as if she could see the stars through the ceiling.

"I figured there was something wrong with me and I needed to fix it. I didn't date for like three years. Then I met Corey, this long-haired pothead who stepped over ants on the sidewalk. He just wouldn't give up. So I gave in. After three months I thought, *Shit, this isn't it either. I'm not feeling what everyone says I'm supposed to. I'm not ready yet.* So I really got into biking, being a courier. I loved the speed, the adrenalin. And then I met Ben."

I poured another shot for each of us. I sat down on the floor beside her.

"Do you remember that day I was bleeding like a pig? I thought I was dying. When Ben showed up at the clinic, I had this overwhelming feeling. All hot and mushy and connected to him. My crotch was pulsing. I thought, *Wow, this must be what love feels like.* Must've been my hormones

— completely out of whack."

There was a long silence. What was I supposed to say? She was playing with the diamond that had replaced Hamlet. Not quite a square, but big enough to put a dent in photography school. The band was white gold.

"Lie down on your back," she said.

"What?"

"C'mon. Last wish."

I lay down. She straddled me and whipped off her top.

"Gaineil!"

Then her bra was off, and she leaned over me so our faces were almost touching.

"Look." We both stared at her dangling breasts. Two stemless wineglasses. She jiggled, but they didn't move much. Then she grabbed them the way she grabs Harpo's paws and forces him to dance. We cackled uncontrollably.

"Check this out," she said, sitting back, the full weight of her pelvis balanced on my thighs. Her brown nipples, two points on a map. She closed her eyes, then moved like a jackhammer, giggling even though I'd stopped.

Harpo had been lying down in the corner but he appeared beside us now, looking up at Gaineil's face. His nose twitched. *Is she playing? Does she need help?* His tail a random metronome. Then he stood completely still, his body tense, ready. Both of us staring at Gaineil.

She kept her eyes closed so long I began to feel absurd. Then she suddenly cradled her breasts like the lead in a tasteful porn movie. That moment in the scene when you know the actress is just a girl with skills, good at making everyone — the cameraman, the director, the temporary lover — disappear.

VIOLETTA

Chloe hangs Bert's clothes on the line. She has no clothespins, just hooks the shirts under the armpits.

Violetta calls out to her, Canna you move you recycling bin?

Oh, is it in the way again? As if she didn't know.

The dog, he no bark so much no more. Her index finger, an arthritic hook, pointing to Baxter. His coat looking richly chocolate today in the sun, lying in his usual position, ball in mouth, the ever-ready retriever.

Look atta this. She points to the driveway.

What?

The tree. Ev'ry day I sweep. Shit. Today I watcha the wind. Lassa night I can't sleep. I think about the tree. Is so big. I call the city so many times to cut. Nothing.

Chloe just nods when she doesn't understand.

She lights a cigarette. Violetta coughs. As usual she's in the farthest corner of her porch, sitting at the round table just big enough to hold her Bible, ahem-ing at the sound of Chloe's lighter, even though the wind's not going her way.

The shirts are men doubled over, caught in barbed wire. Chloe once rode her bicycle fast into a clothesline, turning her head to yell at Baxter. There was no laundry, no warning, just pegs, the old-fashioned wooden kind, heads bobbing, legs clutching the line, not letting go even on contact. The impact of a guillotine. She had marks on her neck, a red beaded choker, for a month.

Signora. You take. Violetta waves at her parsley in a pot. Too much this year.

Violetta's pots are lined up along the railing of her wooden porch. Geraniums, cucumber, tomatoes, sweet peppers, chives. When Chloe sits in any one of the four garden chairs around her tiny backyard table and looks towards Violetta, alone in her chair on the porch, she sees Violetta's head as a pot.

My sister, she sick. In Milano. Cancer. And she putta the heart. Lassa year. Electric. To pumpa, you know?

Oh. I'm sorry. Are you close?

Huh?

Are you close with your sister?

Violetta's eyebrows cave in, her mouth tight at the end of her sentences. Except now, when she genuinely doesn't understand, her face is open, and Chloe sees the young woman who came with her husband to Toronto so long ago.

Um, are you near to her?

Huh, yeah. She before me. One year. But she got lotsa

problems. Like me. Heh-heh. My hip is no so good. It hurt to do things. I do everything by myself. I alone. 'S just me.

Violetta's been alone for the five years Chloe's owned her half of the semi. Violetta's husband went back to Italy fifteen years ago, and died there. No kids. No pets. Just plants that sometimes surprise — *the tomatoes, not so good this-a year* — and a constant stream of old Italian couples popping in before and after church, the husbands helping out with man jobs. The occasional game of cards on the porch with another widow. Black cardigans over their shoulders, the limp woollen arms flapping as they discard and pick up from the deck.

Violetta's hair is short, like all the Catholic ladies. She gets it styled every week and comes home looking even tighter. By the end of the day, Chloe sees that it's brushed out, the cowlick stubborn. Like Violetta. When she cocks her head to tell about someone on the street who is sick or dying, Chloe checks the eyes behind the big square frames. The brown specks in her irises magnified. *Is that a tear?* Then she remembers Violetta's harsh words. *Why you don' clean you backyard? You don' do nothing. You fat. You maybe eat too much.*

Every morning at dawn, *shwook, shwook,* Violetta sweeps her driveway, the sidewalk. Except when her hip is bad. Those mornings Chloe lies in her bed at the front of the house, picturing the old woman lying in her bed. One wall and forty years separating them.

The previous owner had told her that Frank, Violetta's husband, used to give it to her every single night. Chloe imagines lying still next to the perfect rhythm of the knocking headboard, rooting for Frank to come quickly for

Violetta's sake. With Bert, Chloe had pressed her face into the pillow, knowing the neighbourhood listened, knowing she went on too long. She even shushed Bert in his moment of climax. That sleepless summer of his death, she often heard a woman's pleasurable moan from somewhere on Manning. Was it Fiorenza or Georgina or Anna? One quick cry like a bullet through her open bedroom window.

Cecile, who lives one street over, told her about the year Frank died in Milan. Violetta's hair turned completely white, but she looked ten years younger. She no longer peered out from behind the screen door. She walked to the shops on College Street, wore pants, planted geraniums, and occasionally smiled.

The sun is strong. Violetta is eyeing the shirts on Chloe's line. They're going to Goodwill today. She had finally found the strength to go through Bert's closet. When he died, the empty house filled up with land mines. The end of the brown leather sofa, sunken from his nightly position under the reading lamp; an unread *Maclean's* on his desk; the bookmark in Grisham's latest, page 139. Four used tea bags lined up on the kitchen windowsill, that he'd saved for the garden. Each crinkled brown sac deflated. She caught herself listening for the creak of the screen door.

That first week, a rectangular package had appeared on her doorstep. Addressed to *Cloy*. On the spine in blue pen: *Hymns (Violetta plays accordion and sings)*. She read the first two titles. "I Know It Was the Blood for Me" and "He Brings Me to the Banquet Table." At first Violetta sounded far away, the accordion loud and close to the mike. Chloe could hear the bellows wheeze, Violetta's fingers hesitating, searching, before stretching over the keys. Eventually the Italian lyrics increased in volume, Violetta's voice weak, like a horse coming up from behind. She'd heard the accordion through the walls, thought, *Surely that's a record.* Who translated the titles for her, for me? Chloe wondered.

Chloe eyes Bert's brown and black checked shirt flopped over the line, the one with the Western collar and white snap buttons, the one he often changed into after work. It needs mending. She remembers lying on top of him on the couch, pressing her ear to his chest. Asking him to tell her about his day, his words like waves in a seashell. Her head rising and falling with each breath. Listening to the sound of his heart, as if she could catch the irregularity, the arrhythmia that would eventually kill him. Her earring caught on the pocket and she shot up in a moment of panic, feeling the sharp tug. Chloe held on to her ear, fearing it would rip. The pocket tearing instead.

She brings her sewing kit out to the backyard. Baxter stops chewing to watch her. The two of them practically live out here. Bert's clothes are stuffed into green garbage bags by the fence, ready to be put in the car. She imagines all those arms and torsos and necks entangled, his dress shirts with his casual. His paint shirts, camping shirts, all unable to breathe in there. She forces herself to see just the bags. Tries to picture herself putting them in the trunk, leaving them at the drop box, driving away. Maybe she'll bring them into the house. Maybe she'll wait.

Violetta goes in and out of her back door all day long, sometimes talking to her, sometimes staying silent. She drops her voice to talk about the family directly behind, who haven't fixed their part of the walkway. She tells Chloe that fat Stefano must be on holiday because his lights stay on all night, that Leo's wife left for another woman, that she knows it's Voula throwing bread in the park for the dirty pigeons.

One day in July, a parade came by their house, a Madonna and a few saints with open arms carried on platforms by adolescent boys, proud in their first role as men. Groups of women, stout like Violetta, strolling, their practised hymns strong and clear. Little girls dressed like angels, halos askew, scanning the crowd for familiar faces. Bored teenage girls with push-up bras and tight tanks under open robes, their mouths barely ajar in song. Priests trying to stay focused on hymn books right behind.

Violetta, excited, hung over her porch railing like a kid. It come lassa year up Beatrice, no here. This year it come-a by here. Santo Jerome. He take-a the . . . the . . . nail out. Of the lion, y'know? Ev'ry year he cutta the finger.

Chloe nodded.

Yeah. Violetta smiled, thinking she was understood.

The following year Violetta invited her in for the first time. The day before the Good Friday procession — the Passion of Christ. There were seven Jesuses in the parade, but the crucified one lived on their street. He had been playing the bloodied, tortured role for twenty years.

My husband, he wassa friend with Jesus. I have the Madonna. You come-a see.

Chloe went around the fence, up the perfectly swept driveway, onto the wooden porch and into the kitchen, expecting a small statue, maybe one Violetta had bought for Easter. The smell of garlic and old furniture hit her. The place was dark, as Chloe had imagined, but there were no flowery embroidered pictures or Italian landscapes on the walls. Just crucifixes. Christ with his head lolling on his right shoulder, Christ with his head up towards God, eyes closed, eyes open, blood, no blood. Violetta could get a good price for that retro kitchen table and chairs.

Violetta ushered her towards the living room. Set up around the periphery were a brown couch and three armchairs with flattened foam cushions. In the centre, a life-size Disneyfied Madonna sat on a platform of plastic flowers, her long baby blue gown in permanent folds. Jesus, a robust toddler, teetered eternally on her lap.

Violetta stood admiring, Chloe knowing to do the same.

Is the Madonna, y'know?

Yeah.

The big one.

Chloe nodded.

Frank, he knew Jesus. The guy carry the cross, y'know? Violetta looked at her and they both laughed.

Chloe stayed gazing at Mary until she knew Violetta was satisfied.

Chloe's sewing the pocket of the checked shirt. It's mid-morning, her favourite time in the backyard, when the parked cars have left for work, the business-suited neighbours have rushed up Manning, coffee Thermoses in hand, to catch the streetcar on College. Violetta's sewing too, on her porch.

You know, when I first come here, I sew. In a factory. In the place, I sew up pantyhose, up the middle — zip-zip. Her fingers two V's.

Oh, really.

Yeah. I sew da package.

Chloe often thinks she's understood Violetta, then realizes no.

Yeah. Then I quit because a the smell. It bother me, y'know? Then I make-a the toy for the baby. But I fall. On the stair. Thatsa why my hip is like this. I hit my head. I no work again. Not for seventeen year. Heh-heh.

Violetta looks up from her sewing. Y'know Cecile? She's inna Spain.

Yeah, she's in Spain right now. Costa Del Sol.

She's a bitch.

What?

She's a bitch.

She's a bitch?

Yeah. She is?

Uh, I don't know.

Yeah, I think so.

Cecile is away until the end of the week, but as soon as Chloe sees her in the dog park with her German shepherd, Sonny, she tells her what Violetta said, because dog people stick together. Once Violetta phoned the police about Sonny's nonstop barking while Cecile was at work.

Cecile doesn't do anything for a couple of days. But on a Saturday morning Chloe sees her walking up Violetta's front steps, ready to take her on. Loud voices through the wall, then nothing for a long while. Chloe goes out to sit in the sun, thankful it's not her in there. The back door swings open.

"*Ciao, signora,*" Violetta says. Cecile comes over to the fence, grinning, leans in to tell Chloe: "Beach, not bitch. I was in Spain, at the beach."

After that Chloe notices more pots on the ledge. So many she can hardly tell when Violetta is there or not. Sometimes she hears the screen door and she looks up and sees no one. Other times Chloe stands up to peer over and Violetta is there, head down in her Bible.

She knows she has made a mistake. Cecile lives down the street, but Violetta is her neighbour. She has formed the wrong alliance.

One day Violetta ends the silence.

You know what happened to the tomato?

No, what? Chloe is relieved she's talking again, gets ready to hear about this year not being a good crop, too small.

You dunno?

No.

Someone taking my tomato.

Really?

Yeah, someone steal my tomato.

Oh, no, Chloe thinks. *Is this my destiny too, alone, with no one to keep paranoia in check?*

Who do you think is taking them? she asks. Who would take your tomatoes?

I think you.

What?

I think you steal my tomato.

Why would I do that, Violetta?

I dunno. Or maybe you dog.

Baxter?

He go up to the plant and take, like that. Maybe he eat the tomato.

I don't think he likes tomatoes.

Anyway, you take them. I know.

Chloe is shaking. Bert's dying has made everything precarious. Locked doors, windows, and fences — the idea of security has become an absurd concept. And now this. She needs some things to never change. Like her neighbours. She's been careful to keep up a public face. Afraid she might scream or cry or lie down and give up, right there in the street. She stares at Baxter. He locks eyes with her, but his mouth is busy gnawing a tennis ball. It's just her now, doing everything.

Violetta spends the next week silent, scowling at Chloe when she comes into the backyard. It's the end of August, the air show is on. Chloe has no experience with war, except on TV. She hears the roar of planes midday and suddenly feels dread.

She looks up and sees nothing. Just the treetops. *Jets are faster than sound*, she thinks. She pictures Violetta's husband flying home to the old country, never coming back. How much longer will it be like this, she wonders, things changing in an instant, sending her headlong into fear? She decides Violetta must be a good person because she nurtures her plants. She has found the desire to grow tomatoes, even without Frank there to eat them. Chloe thinks about tomatoes. How one day they're green and the next they're red. How mysterious that is.

She hasn't made a proper meal for herself since Bert died. Cans of soup, tuna, sardines on toast. Anything that doesn't keep her in the kitchen too long, aware that Bert's not there chopping, sautéing garlic and onion, tea towel over his shoulder. Some nights she finds the energy to make a salad with whatever's about to go mouldy.

A tomato. That's what she needs. She's a condemned woman anyway. She might as well look after herself. It's late, already dark, and she turns out her kitchen light, steps into the backyard. No lights at Violetta's. She's probably in bed or at a church function.

The plant is taller than the half-fence. Violetta has tied it to a stake with pillowcase strips. Chloe plucks the reddest, roundest, ripest tomato she sees. Its spindly stalk snaps easily. She puts it to her nose, relishing the smell. She looks up again towards Violetta's house and sees the widow's shadowed figure on the porch, sitting in the chair in the corner, her head not in her Bible but facing the garden.

Chloe can't see Violetta's expression. For a moment she thinks to put it back. But she knows now that some things can't be reversed. She goes into the house, places it on her cutting board, and cuts it into slices thick as medals.

ENCOUNTER

The ad for the speed-dating event lands in her email inbox.
SUBJECT: *Cna ouy dera htsi?*

> Olny 55 plepoe can raed tihs. The phaonmneal pweor of the hmuan mnid, aoccdrnig to rscheearch at Cmabrigde Uinervtisy, it dseno't mtaetr in what oerdr the ltteres in a wrod are, the olny iproamtnt tihng is taht the frsit and lsat ltteer be in the rghit pclae.

The ad is targeting word geeks, crossword addicts, bookworms, lit lovers like Jill. She thinks, *Why not?*
Now she sits in the chi-chi bar, waiting for the bell to ring, for the steady stream of three-minute encounters.
There's the standard get-to-know-you questions. "What

book is on your bedside table?" "What book has changed your life?" Then there's Lee, who asks, "So why are you still single?"

Jill feels the guilt of her forty years, the cross on her back. *Because I want to make my own bloody life and I just need to get past these next few years of cultural pressure, those smug married people with their "C'mon over to our side, it's wonderful" smiles. To give myself permission to finally leave the party.*

Lee's a skinny guy. He works for the *Toronto Star*, and at first Jill circles YES next to his name on the Speed Date sheet, but at the end of the night she looks at her decisions. She's circled five other YESes and they are hunky guys. Two private investigators; another owns three houses. She looks around at the men scattered at tables, marking their Speed Date sheets, and thinks how unfair it is to pick a guy because he works somewhere she wants to work. She puts a thick black X through Lee's YES and circles NO a bunch of times as if she's circling a track.

It turns out that Toronto Star Guy is her only match. The email comes the next day. She emails the speed-dating coordinator. *Are you sure?* Jill asks her to check if she's missed any of the hunks. No. Toronto Star Guy's the only one who picked her, and Jill has definitely circled YES.

Jill arranges to meet Lee. She's nervous, because she's always nervous before she goes out to meet a man. The hair's not right, the jeans don't fit, she needs new shoes — till she can't even get out the door because her self-concept is doing the *Why bother?* dance. But this night, Pastor's words come to her and she asks Jesus to help her out the door.

She's walking down College Street with Jesus. He's in his

long white robe, the one He always wears, with the dolman sleeves and the gold rope belt. He's wearing the crown of thorns and there's even a bit of blood dripping on His forehead, and then there's not, because Jill wants to keep it happy. The two of them are swinging joined hands like two friends in the playground. On Sunday Pastor says he prays to Jesus as if He's a friend. A friend who always comes when he calls. "Nothing's too small for prayer," Pastor says.

Jesus, just hold my hand to the coffee shop, just get me there without once saying I'm not worthy.

At Café Luna, when she sees Toronto Star Guy, she lets go, because Toronto Star Guy is human. So human. Kind of nervous looking and tired in his navy windbreaker, looking as skinny as she remembers.

They sit and Jill fluffs the left side of her hair because that side always goes flat, and after all, he's still a guy and she wants her hair to be right so he'll have no excuse to reject her before she makes a decision.

The waitress starts clicking her pen. Toronto Star Guy asking about lattes. "Is that in a cup or one of those bowls?"

"You can get either."

"Is it the same amount?"

"No, you get more in a bowl."

"Oh, so the cup is like a regular cup?"

"Yep."

"And what's the price difference?"

"I'm not sure. Like eighty cents or something."

"Eighty cents?"

"Yeah. Let me get the menu," the waitress says. And she's looking and she can't find it right away and Jill looks at Toronto Star Guy and sees that the difference between the cup and the bowl is important. And she decides right there this isn't a date, and he decides on decaf because it's late and he has to work the next day. They start talking and they both went to the same university, got the same communications degree, had a lot of the same teachers, and followed a similar path, except Toronto Star Guy gave up his dream of being an editor and took a dead-end job at the paper and Jill is desperately holding on to hers of being an editor. She's staring at his regret and it looks pale and wrinkled and hard, like something you hold on to when the Devil's whispering in your ear.

"It's like our lives have run parallel," he says.

"Have you ever explored religion?" she says.

Pause. Then, "I'm a Christian." He looks at her as if he's confident she won't ask for the bill, like he's taking a chance but he's not too worried.

"I just started going to a *really* Christian church," Jill says.

"Which one?"

"Downtown Church."

"Really? That's my church. I haven't seen you there," he says.

"I've only been going for like five weeks."

"I've missed the past five weeks."

"Wow." It's *aha* for both of them. Jill can finally have a conversation with someone on the inside. She's been dying to do that. And he seems normal.

"You can ask me anything," he says.

He's having a crisis of faith. A mini one, he tells her, but he's a total believer. He was drinking *a lot*, he says. *Before.* The words are like part of a code they already share. He assures her he's never alone now. It's everything they say it is. And then she tells him she asked Jesus to walk down College with her for the first time tonight. Using a voice like she knows what that means.

"Why did you do that?"

"Because I was nervous."

"Why?" He's got his finger pointing at her like an investigator. Like maybe she'll confess her desire for him. Like there's hope for him.

"And who was here?" he says. "Who? Me! That's no coincidence. That's the Holy Spirit. This night is all about you, Jill. *This is your moment.*"

And Jill thinks, *Could the Holy Spirit slip into the coffee shop without me noticing?* Without all the disco lights of Downtown Church and the Hammond organ in D minor.

Jill's laughing because it feels joyous. She remembers the NO she circled on her paper and how God must have changed it to a YES.

She asks him everything. If I'm a Christian will I lose my sense of humour? Will I have to stop saying *fuck*? Will I stop feeling like a walking lint-collector of guilt that I spend each night picking off with a roller brush and reapplying each day? Jill doesn't ask this last thing but she knows this is why she wants to go to the other side. To where those eyes shine, Toronto Star Guy right in the middle.

"Will I walk around seeing everything as a JC sign? How will I get anything done?"

"You can call me twenty-four hours. You have my number." And then he takes her to his car and Jill sits in the bucket seat of his rusted-out Honda and he prays for her. "Thanks, Lord, for this amazing happening."

And Jill bows her head and hears the words "Jesus open her heart so that she may know You," and she practises visualizing her heart opening. And tries not to think of how the words sound like every TV evangelist she's ever switched channels on. She remembers hearing that the human mind does not read every word but absorbs the gist. She thinks how she is one of the fifty-five people in the world who are able to see right through to the message. She thinks how wrong she's been about how a Toronto Star Guy dresses and the kind of expensive car he must drive. She pictures those thoughts leaving her heart so she can make room for the love that will soon come pouring in. Maybe it already has and she just hasn't noticed.

‹ ‹ ‹

Jill goes to a Christian Primary Encounter in a church basement. Eight people show up. They sit at a long table and watch a video, *Who Is the Holy Spirit?* featuring Ricky, a tall born-again with a thick English accent and crisply delivered punch lines. A pork tenderloin dinner is served and they watch another video, *What Does the Holy Spirit Do?* Ricky again, standing in the pulpit of a high-ceilinged church; cut to thoughtful young listeners nodding, well-groomed, taking notes. At the end of each video, the encounter leader in the church basement asks Jill and the others, "What did Ricky say about that?" pretending he's forgotten and needs the group to remember for him.

Then everyone is offered a choice of walnut tart or cherry cheesecake and over coffee, Jill sits next to the encounter leader and his wife. They're smiling so big that she feels compelled to tell them about walking down College with Jesus. As she describes swinging His hand, their cheesecake forks stall in midair and they nod simultaneously, beaming. After the last video, *How Can I Resist Evil?* everyone stands in a circle.

The lights are dimmed and a guy with an electric guitar feeds the words to the group. *You are the breath. Enter. You are welcome. Sweet sweet Lord. Enter.*

Jill closes her eyes in the circle. She can see herself standing, all five feet of her, hands and face up to heaven. She's rolled up the bottoms of her jeans so the Lord can see her suede boots, see that she's soft, ready. Her short hair in two tiny bunches sticking out like paintbrush tips from her neck. Jill relaxes her face, smoothes it out so He'll see her as a lost pixie in the forest and bring her home.

"Anyone feel anything?" the encounter leader says. Right away Jill feels her palms tingle. If she concentrates they get hotter. She keeps the tingle to herself though, listening for the Lord to creep up her arms, slide down into her heart, split open the dam Ricky says is in there.

Jill can hear whispers in a prayer language. She hears the words *JesusJesusJesus* and other sounds like Russian or pig Latin. The woman next to her starts sniffing like she's got a cold, then she's crying like someone hit her. Jill wants to peek but she uses her body as eyes, hears movement in the circle, a whisper, and then she feels a hand on her back and she doesn't flinch because she knows it's the blond girl, the one who giggles a lot and looks like that actress Kirsten Dunst. Whispering in her ear, like an angel perched there.

"Dear Lord, please come and fill Jill with Your spirit. Right here. Let her know Your love. You love her so. She doesn't need to do anything to receive Your love. She is perfect as she is. Open her heart, Lord."

There is a pause and Jill is swaying with two hands on her shoulders now, and the guitar is strumming chords like the part in a movie when the character is running and crying and walking through a lonely city just before a decision.

The sobbing woman beside her is being asked to sit in a chair. Jill hears her blowing her nose. She can hear tongue language from three different places in the circle. She opens her eyes a slit and sees the "believers" standing in front of or behind each of the non-believers, and the non-believers are outnumbered. All this for three of us, Jill thinks. An electric guitar with an amplifier. All for her. She panics a little.

Then she thinks, *They are helping me. They know Jesus has visited me already. They are opening up the heavens so I can enter and they've made stuffed pork tenderloin in a way I never could have cooked for myself. And I've had two slices.*

She's come here tonight knowing this might be her moment. And when the angel says she's perfect just as she is, she feels the way she did when her last boyfriend touched her in almost the right way for her to fly, right there in her own bed, and she wanted to direct him a little to the left.

The angel's voice is crescendoing now. And Jill can picture the pilot light Ricky talked about, the one that burns for all Christians, the light that never goes out once you are born.

"Let her fall, Lord, let her know it's safe. Fill her heart. Even though we don't understand everything, Lord. Let her know this is not a strange thing. There is nothing she needs to do, Lord. Let her breathe in Your love."

Jill's eyes sting. They've told her it's the Holy Spirit when her eyes sting. But she wonders if the angel has been taught to say the right things. Maybe it's not the Lord. But what if it's the Lord working through the angel's words and He's trying to heal her right now?

Then there's a second voice in front of her. A woman holding her forearms like it's a partner stretch at the Y. "Please, God. Jill is beautiful and smart and talented." And Jill's thinking, *How do you know?* Jill's thinking this angel is not as good. Hasn't trained as long as the other one. "Give her the free gift You are offering: eternal life."

Jill breathes so the hands on her shoulders can feel she's doing what she's been asked. She's trying. She's really trying. But she knows it's too late because the picture of her pilot light goes out. Her hands are tingling. Because she's been holding them up for so long or because Jesus is tapping on the door, and she's disappointed for the angels because the angels don't know it's too late.

Jill feels her brain standing guard there in her head. Her brain saying *home*, and Jill grabs on to the word the way you grab on to a pillow and decide to sleep right there on the floor, knowing you'll be comfortable where you are, you don't need to go up to the guest room and see the tiny pink soap and the fresh towel waiting just for you. The pillow will be enough until you can get to your own bed, thank you.

The angels are swaying and Jill's not sure if she herself is standing straight up anymore. Jill makes one final attempt, for the good angel's sake. She imagines her body staying and the rest of her like the outside of a wheat husk winnowed out and up and floating big, looking down, but it's like trying too hard to have an orgasm, going through a Rolodex of fantasies that just aren't catching.

And she feels the giggle in her belly, in her throat, and she lets it come, giving the angels a smile so they know she's at least opened a little. "Thank you, Lord," the good angel says and Jill opens her eyes and hugs her. Looks for disappointment in the angel's eyes. There's none, Jill thinks, because the woman beside her cried and had to have a chair, and she's the one who got saved, the lamb offered in place of Jill tonight. Jill is grateful to the crying lamb.

"It's just not my time." Jill's learned her part of the script from she doesn't know where. And she walks home and asks for a thirst, as Ricky on the video told her to do. A thirst so the Lord can satisfy.

‹ ‹ ‹

The next day she wakes up and her day feels different. Jill rides the streetcar to work. Her Bible tucked inside a magazine. Christ is feeding the masses but it looks like *Vogue*. She imagines the day she'll say in the church basement circle, *I remember when I couldn't hold my hands up in church. I remember hiding my Bible on the bus like an early-morning purchase from the liquor store.*

On her walk from the streetcar she actually looks into people's eyes as they pass. And they look back. As if she is actually visible and making a difference with her eyes.

Then the lady she buys her latte and doughnuts from every morning says, "You're amazing!"

"Yeah?"

"You've got fives — I needed fives!" *Loaves and fishes*, Jill wants to say.

Loaves and fishes. Even the homeless man heading for breakfast, roll of sleeping bag under his armpit, stops mid-cough to smile at her. *Maybe it's my miniskirt and knee-high boots*, she thinks.

She's walked along Hilton Street a hundred early mornings before, going over the list of stuff to do the minute she gets in the office. Today she sees each house. Doors with stained glass eyes or dented brown screens or else stone-arched like Snow White's cottage. Winding shrub-lined paths, crooked steps, precise concrete porches, overflowing recycling bins, wind chimes no one is awake to hear. The long-stemmed pink, purple, and white flowers, daisy witch hair, laughing in the wind at the lack of garden plan. How could she not have noticed these before? The only flowers still alive this late in the fall. And the lavender-painted house opposite the bright purple. Like two perfect sisters. Jill feels a jolt of energy as she passes between them. And then the tiny shrine behind a low iron fence, Mary's long blue gown, hands open, head down. A ceramic plaque by a door, the calm face of Jesus. How could she have walked by these?

At work the coffee isn't brewed yet. The files she needs are not on her desk and when people sleepwalk through her good morning, she understands. She knows this is what those shining-faced other-siders experience 24/7. She gets it.

At ten thirty she tells Jesus to take a break. She won't be one of those instant salvations. She's tasted it and she's putting her fork down to see if it comes back. Jill wants it to be like a visit to the optometrist, clicking those two lenses around and around until the bottom row is clearly black. And then she'll feel shame for reciting B-M-G-N-L-R all along, when now she clearly sees P-N-O-M-L-B.

‹ ‹ ‹

In church the Sunday after disappointing the angels, Jill stands in the front pew of the school auditorium with all the families and couples. She has been coming long enough to know she is one of a handful of single people in the congregation. When they all raise their hands to Jesus, Jill spreads her fingers wide like nets. The Christian rock group plays onstage. The keyboardist with his hair full of product, his tanning-booth owl eyes. The drummer behind Plexiglas, the bass guitarist, two backup girls on mikes swaying and keeping their eyes on God. The huge electric blue video screen, hymn lyrics in flashes of pink. Back wall a swirl of disco lights.

The congregation is clapping and moving. *I am free. Free to dance. Turn around.* The whole auditorium, suits and dresses, is jumping, and Jill jumps along like a teenager at a punk rock concert, turning around and around on the chorus. They do this for a solid hour, until Pastor Steve takes the mike and walks across the stage, his steps punctuated by the electronic keyboard, slowing its tempo to match his pace. Jill looks for Toronto Star Guy but she can't quite recall what he looks like.

Pastor Steve is on fire today. His fox face is boyish, his double-breasted suit perfectly pressed, neck skin bulging a little over the collar. He's talking about Women of Impact. The book of Ruth. How she did what wasn't expected of her. Not what people told her to do. She was an unmarried woman in a foreign land. Open to judgement. But she did what God wanted her to do. And the best part is, all women have that power. To not engage in men-bashing. To not engage in the killing of hundreds of thousands of babies each year.

And Jill starts to hear the power of the word. The very words she's skimmed over in hopes of hearing the bigger message.

"We wouldn't kill a baby on the outside, so why is it all right to kill a baby on the inside?" Ruth eventually returned to her home and married. Pastor Steve talks about the covenant of marriage. Has not the Lord made them one? In flesh and spirit they are His. And why one? Because He is seeking godly offspring.

"But don't worry." Pastor Steve smiles. "He would never ask you to marry someone you weren't attracted to." The congregation chuckles. One collective chuckle.

Jill looks at the pastor's eyes. They aren't glistening like last week. They aren't reflecting a curious place.

And when Pastor Steve says, "Let's pray," Jill bows her head. Pastor Steve says, "Anyone who feels Jesus tugging at their hearts today, just raise your hand so I can see you. Just come down to the front so I can meet you. Just come down to the front. And if you're already a Christian and you want to come down and show Him your love today, come down to the front."

Jill keeps her eyes closed in prayer and feels the movement of bodies towards the front, and she keeps her arms out. Waiting for the tingling from last week. But it's cold. She's cold. There's nothing now.

She remembers how, as she climbed out of Toronto Star Guy's car, he expressed concern about the hole his poppy had made in his windbreaker. It might have broken the waterproof seal, he said. And she had a moment of silence for all those soldiers who died so he could have a waterproof jacket at all. And she thinks now that maybe being saved doesn't protect you all that much.

Jill opens her eyes and watches the Christians spring into action, moving the pulpit back to make room for all those seeking salvation, several pastors laying on hands, whispering in ears, holding heads, pressing blessings onto foreheads. She watches the newly saved as they are struck down by Jesus's love. Jill watches a woman sobbing as others fall around her, the Christians catching them swiftly, safely. Some lie flailing, some frozen in various positions as if lightning has struck, and she is safe in her wooden pew. She watches the pastor on the microphone pacing frantically onstage, speaking in tongues, as if he's returned to his homeland. *JesusJesusJesus*. Jill watches the pastors and their wives as they lay on hands, watches to maybe see where their eyes have gone, to catch a hint of pretend. But their faces are earnest, driven with purpose.

"Jill."

She turns to her left. And she sees one of the head preachers, the one with the nice thick hair, coming towards her with his beautiful wife. She sees her pew is empty. Entirely empty. She looks behind her and sees most of the pews are empty. She is standing alone in the second row with her arms out and this head preacher, whom she's never met, is coming down the pew, calling her name.

"You know the Lord, right?" He places his hand on her back.

Jill says yes but she knows she'll only disappoint.

"Let me pray for you. Lord, I feel that Jill has been struggling alone for a long time now. Lord, come into her heart. Into her life. That she may know You. In relationship. I feel that she has struggled with relationships, Lord. Come that she may . . . relationship." He's missing words, he's bumbling through, he's in his fervour. Jill can hear him loud and fast, heading for a quick climax. His hand shaking on her shoulder.

"I feel great fire from you, Jill."

Jill keeps her arms wide just in case. But she can't seem to close her eyes with the preacher because she sees that the Christians in front of her are moving quickly to lay forest green blankets on the falling saved, plush green blankets with rounded corners and finished edges of plump silk piping. Fine piping. Someone has taken the time to sew these blankets for just such an occasion. Jill sees they are just the size to cover a waist or a torso or two legs, or a gaping wound. She focuses on the green, the garden of thick moss, familiar and binding, not large enough to let anyone get too comfortable down there.

SPEARS

After what happened, Jane made a list of all the things she'd killed when she was young. Eight green frogs at the cottage, hung like mittens on the clothesline. The sparrow knocked out by her bedroom window kept in a shoebox without air holes — Jane and her brother watched its chest heave like her dad's cheeks on the harmonica until it stopped, its frantic eye finally shut down. The fly de-winged with her mom's expensive tweezers, dancing in simulated takeoff. All these crimes were executed with her brother, true, but they were enjoyed and fully participated in by Jane just the same. And then there was Blackie, the retriever her dad loved more than her. She left the door open at least a half-dozen times, whispered descriptions of cliffs, the lapping waves of Labrador, saying, "Go home." One day he ran away for good.

She made this list the way a jury scrutinizes character, looking for clues.

It was late in the day when they arrived at what they thought was an empty campsite. They'd had a relaxed start but were late meeting Rachel. Robby had wanted to buy a fishing rod when they stopped for breakfast in Huntsville. He'd never been canoeing before, only car camping with his mom, and Jane wanted to keep her new boyfriend's son happy.

Canisbay was the first lake inside Algonquin Park, a nice easy introduction, no portaging. They met the Canoe Lake van in the parking lot, picked up their three-man canoe, and transferred their gear from the car, intending to head out on the lake straight away. But Robby was hungry. *The kid's always hungry*, Jane thought as they unpacked their food sack on the grass by the lake. She'd seen the routine with Vasco. "Pasta and cheese? Ham? Hummus? What about that meatloaf you like?" Robby sitting at the table, scissoring his legs with each no until Vasco gave in to Pizza Pops, yet again.

If it were up to her, he'd be getting his own lunch as soon as he was old enough to say the word. Twelve was too late. "Making sandwiches is no fun, so why have no fun?" he'd say.

"A miniature Woody Allen," she had described him to Rachel. "You have to come. I need a buffer. You need a break. Please?"

Jane and Rachel, best friends since grade school. Rachel was coming out of a nasty breakup with Doug. His ex had showed up with a surprise, demanding child support, threatening to move to Newfoundland. Rachel hadn't spoken to him since the DNA tests and his move down east, where he was spending a lot of money fighting for visitation rights.

Jane watched as Rachel laid out her straw mat and her dachshund, Rufus, promptly curled up for a nap. Robby was eating a boiled egg, the same shape as his head. His black curls an add-on, a Mr. Potato Head accessory. Maybe that was the key: give him things the shape of his skull. He had that little bottle of antiseptic in his pocket, his hands peeling from washing them so much. She didn't tell him about the eggshell clinging to his thumbnail.

"Robby, are you excited about the trip?" Rachel asked.

"Yeah. I'm going to catch a fish. My dad once caught a fish *this big*."

Rachel said, "Really?"

Jane shook her head behind his back. Vasco was not a fisherman. That was part of her appeal, she knew. Well-travelled, outdoorsy. She looked at the lake. It was choppy. Late August, a few trees starting to turn, the sun still hot.

"I need my sunscreen," Robby said. *The kid's got it all covered*, Jane thought.

"Where is it?" he asked.

"In your blue bag, I think. Where's your blue bag?"

"I don't know. And I need my hat. I think I left it in the car."

The beach of overturned rental canoes, all yellow. *The colour of something beginning*, Jane thought. She watched a couple put on life jackets and head out for a leisurely day paddle. The tight-bodied woman in a tank top and yoga pants that showed off her figure. One of the benefits of not having kids. That's what Jane would be wearing if Vasco were here, loading a picnic lunch into the hull. She'd pull her long red hair back, leave a few sexy tendrils. She'd let Vasco steer. Her in the bow with all that water and day before her. Vasco watching her strong profile, sturdy chin, the muscles in her back with each stroke. Determined to have Vasco all to herself.

"Rufy, want some?"

"Um, Robby, I don't feed Rufy human food," Rachel said.

"Rufy, want some?" He was holding out part of a carrot.

"Robby," Jane said.

"Rufy . . ." Waving it in front of his nose.

"*Robby!*"

"Okay!"

Why had she agreed to this? Vasco was at the airport this weekend. He was a ground-based air traffic controller. This was all so new. She pictured him, lone man on the runway, the reflector lines of his vest elongating his torso, his arms waving a trusted code.

The first campsites they canoed past were all taken.

"Is that one?" Robby pointing to the orange triangular symbol on a distant tree.

"It's taken. See the canoe?"

"They don't give out more permits than sites. Don't worry," Rachel said.

"I'm not worried," Robby said, holding on to Rufy. He hadn't let go of him since they got in the canoe.

"Did you hear the girl at the permit office? She said a bear wandered into camp last night," Jane said.

"Maybe we should just go home."

"That's in the car camping area, Robby," Rachel said.

As a distraction, Jane took the Walmart fishing rod out of its plastic container, fitted the top part into the base, and threaded the line through the steel loops. The lure was a tuft of red and black feathers, and she tied it to the hook like it was a tiny dead bird. Robby smiled as he dropped it right next to him in the water, pulling on the wire until it trailed out behind the canoe. Jane watched him repeatedly lift it up to disappointment. He tried moving his arm like a baseball throw to outfield but the hook flopped close to the boat each time.

"Here, let me try," Rachel said.

Robby ignored her, slicing the rod through the air. It caught on something and the spool seized. His hands held up an Etch-a-Sketch jumble of line, seaweed dripping like hair.

"Great. Now what? What a piece of crap." He threw the rod into the boat, crossed his arms, pulled his hat over his eyes, and leaned back on his rolled-up sleeping bag.

Jane turned her mind to wine. Riesling. True, it was a Tetra Pak box, but it was Riesling just the same. They found a site near the end of the lake, bursting with pine trees. Jane docked the canoe between two fallen trunks. They heard noises, kids' voices. Three boys came through the tiny clearing at the water's edge, holding long pointed sticks.

"Are you guys camping here?" Jane called out.

"Nah, we're just sharpening our spears."

"I'm Oscar." The voice was teenager crackly but the kid was no older than Robby.

Robby stared at their sticks.

"This is Robby," Jane said.

"You have the best rocks. Mind if we use them?" Oscar was a little man. His body seemed to have stopped growing, as if it had said to his large head, *Go on without me*. His shoulders went too far out over the width of him. His arms hung like a shirt on a clothesline.

Jane slung her leg over the side as anchor.

"Can I help?" Oscar moved closer to the shore. The light glowed red through his protruding ears. Without waiting for her to secure the boat, Robby stepped out from the middle. Rufy leaped after him, almost capsizing them all.

As Jane and Rachel unloaded the canoe, Robby watched the boys scrape the ends of their sticks on the rocks surrounding the firepit. The three of them were right out of an old black-and-white movie, the freckle-faced ringleader and his two grubby, grass-stained sidekicks, bracing the branches under their well-worn flip-flops. Scraping intently with perfectly chosen stones.

"This is Max and Jeff." When Oscar talked, the skin on his face seemed to stretch with each word. "They're brothers." They didn't make eye contact with Jane, but she didn't mind. It was Oscar who interested her. She could see what he would look like forty years from now.

"Who are you camping with?"

"Our dads. We come here for a week every summer."

"The same campsite?"

"Yep." He pointed to a trail leading into thick brush. "We have a big cook tent and my dad makes really good mac and cheese," Oscar said. "Have you found your treasure box yet?"

"No." Robby pouted. He'd almost backed out when he heard there were no flush toilets.

"It's way better than an outhouse."

Oscar plonked himself on a log by the firepit, glancing at Max and Jeff as they wandered away on the skinny footpath into the woods.

"Shouldn't you be getting back too, Oscar? It's almost seven o'clock."

"Nah. Dad hasn't even started dinner."

"So where are you from, Oscar?"

"We used to live in Brantford but my mom and dad got divorced. My dad got depressed so now we're moving in with my Auntie Linda in Toronto. That's my dad's sister. She's a nurse and she's got lots of friends."

"What does your dad do?"

"He's an electrician, and my mom says he makes so much money he doesn't know what to do with it, so she's going to ask him to buy her a bigger house. So I can have a bigger bedroom and a tree house and stuff."

"Is there any ginger ale?" Robby asked.

"The cooler's over there," Jane said, holding up her glass of Riesling.

Robby looked at the blue box by the tree, then sat staring into the empty campfire site.

The wine was draining pretty quickly, Rachel and Jane tag-teaming questions, Jane figuring she would quit when Oscar stopped answering, but he never did.

"Are there any women at your campsite, Oscar?"

"Just Rebecca. She's Frank's girlfriend."

"Does your dad have a hatchet? We forgot to bring one," Jane said. Rachel looked at her, knowing they had a hatchet, knowing what Jane was up to.

"For sure. Do you want me to ask if you can borrow it?"

"We could come and get it. We need to collect some wood in the forest anyway," Jane said.

"We'll get you some wood," Oscar said, his face lighting up. "C'mon, Robby. We can hunt bears."

Robby was picking up rocks, stalling.

"Go on, Robby. Go," Jane said.

"Why don't you take one of the walkie-talkies?" Rachel said. Jane felt bad. She should have thought of that.

"We can be spies," Robby said.

"No, so we know where you are," Jane said. Robby looked down at the ground. "Who pissed in your cornflakes? When I call you, answer, so I know you're okay." She had to at least pretend to be a parent.

"Okay."

"I'll protect him." Oscar stood, raised his spear and looked into Jane's eyes as if heading off to explore the Americas. Then both boys disappeared into the corridor of pines.

"Be back by dark, Robby," Jane called.

"Rufy! Stay. Good boy. Dogs are so much easier, eh?" Rachel said.

Rachel and Jane puttered. They set up the tent, started a fire, propped a log between two rocks for a makeshift table, refilled their glasses.

"Nice kid, that Oscar," Jane said.

"Boys with spears. Do you think Robby's okay with them?"

"Sure," Jane answered quickly. "Y'know that summer when I went to Kenya? We saw lots of Masai warriors. Our bus would be rolling along the savannah and we'd come across a huge open-air market. Each vendor was selling the same things — red tartans, sandals made from rubber tires. And long, hollowed-out gourds to carry lion's blood. The Masai drink it. When you go into the Orongoro Crater on safari, you're all in Jeeps. But the Masai can walk right into the valley because they're protected. The lions smell their own blood."

"Hmm. Maybe that's what we need to do with men."

"So they won't know we're coming?"

"So they won't think we're the enemy." Jane wrapped three potatoes in foil and placed them in the centre of the fire, where the coals pulsed. "One night we camped and there was a Masai who lived in a tent on the edge of the campground. He was our security guard. Apparently some locals would rip everything off our backs if we gave them the chance. He went on duty at sunset. And get this, he only had a spear."

"Was his name Oscar?"

"Ha! So of course I need to go to the bathroom in the middle of the night. I get up in the dark, scared shitless, mostly because I don't want to bump into the Masai guy. I decide not to go to the actual toilets, so I pee in the dark, away from the tents and the nightlight from the john. I'm squatting and scanning around for our guard and I never see him. I'm thinking, *Maybe he's like the security guards at home, asleep in his tent*. The campsite is dead quiet. And I suddenly realize we're not protected at all.

"And I think, *Where the fuck am I? Who cares if I live or*

die? What am I doing so far from home? The next morning I ask our guide where the Masai guy was last night. And you know what he said? 'The fact you didn't see him, madam, means he is very good at his job. You didn't see him because he was there.'"

"Did you believe him?"

"How was I to know? That's the thing when you're so far from home. You have to trust someone."

"Here's to trusting someone," Rachel said sarcastically.

Jane put three burgers on the grill over the fire. The two of them reclined in camp chairs, clutching plastic cups as if piloting a plane, navigating through sparks and the lick of flames.

"Wonder what the spears are like at the other site."

"You've already got one. It's me that should be looking."

"Let's go next door and ask to borrow a cup of Coleman fuel."

"Because we're cooking."

"And we're hot, hot, hot. Ha! I wonder if Oscar looks like his dad," Jane said.

"I wonder if Oscar's dad looks like Oscar. I'll bet Oscar is the adult in that relationship."

"You got that too, eh?"

"I mean, it's almost creepy, being that polite."

"Probably goes to boarding school, home for Christmas and Easter. It's perfect."

Jane pulled out the jar of mayonnaise. "Smell it. Spoiled, just like Robby."

They laughed and put their feet up in front of the campfire. The heat coming through Jane's runners. She listened to the gentle knocking of the tied-up canoe, the electric leg-rub of cicadas. Two wolves' call-and-answer. She looked up at the stars, dormant all day, now making an appearance. She watched a bug crawl out of one of the logs, as if running from a burning building. *Things always come to the surface*, she thought.

"It's getting dark." Rachel looked worried.

Jane felt aggravated. She poked one of the potatoes with a fork through the foil.

"Rufy seems content here."

"Did you see how Robby can't let him be a dog? Carries him around like a baby," Jane said. "Probably needs a little brother. Like that's going to happen!"

"What if you had one like Oscar?"

"Oscar, I could handle."

The air suddenly got colder, and Jane and Rachel changed from shorts to long pants and socks to prevent bug bites. Jane put more wood on the fire, her body moving slowly from the wine. The sky dropped into black.

"Hey. Didn't I leave the walkie-talkie right here?"

"I thought I saw it by the tent."

"Shit." Jane got up, stumbled once, the wine working its way through her limbs. "Damn trees. I can't see a thing. Whose idea were trees?"

"Get the Petzl headlamp."

Jane bent over near the fly of the tent.

"Yoo-hoo," Rachel called from the fire. Jane looked up to see her dangling the walkie-talkie by the antenna.

"Who taught you how to hold that thing, girl?"

"Doug . . . *not*."

"Yeah, well look what I got." Jane spun the Petzl headlamp like a bride's garter, let it go so it almost landed in the fire.

"Hey, watch it. We might need that to go on an adventure tonight. I think the burgers are burnt." Rachel handed the walkie-talkie to Jane and grabbed the tongs.

Jane ripped open a bag of chips.

"I guess I should be checking in, eh? Stepmom-of-the-Year Award and all. Robby? Robby?"

"Uh, pressing the button might work."

"Shut up. Robby? Robby, come in. Where are you?"

No response.

"Robby. Robby, can you hear me?"

"Maybe the battery's dead," Rachel said, hugging Rufy.

"Robby?"

Jane sensed a hint of panic in her belly, but her legs felt heavy as she sat in the chair. *What if he doesn't come back?* The thought grew as she stared at the tepee of logs, the flames in a steady dance, the panic overtaking her. Not because Robby was out there somewhere. Not because she couldn't picture him, had no control over the world beyond the fire. But because she didn't feel compelled to look for him. At what point, she wondered, would a mother begin searching?

Jane and Rachel finished the last of the wine. Jane making a pact with herself. *We'll hang the garbage and the food bag in the tree. If he's not back by then, we'll head over to the site.* But it took time to pack the toothpaste, toiletries, dishes, and food into the bag. It took time to find a tree far from their tents with a branch at the right height. It took several tries to toss the rope over. They tied a rock to the end but it kept unravelling with each toss, so they tried a stick that looked like a cross. They wove the yellow rope around it, god's eye. They tried overhand and underhand. And when the sack was dangling like a cocoon, the panic began to envelop her, the way night had settled, making everything feel serious, urgent. The steps she knew should be taken, right this moment. The questions that would later be asked.

When, exactly, did you learn the walkie-talkies didn't work?

She kept her head down, trying to focus the light on her boots. The wine had made her feet feel as if they didn't belong to her. As if the steps were preplanned. Events had already happened. Jane just had to catch up.

Rachel poked apart the logs in the fire until the flames died, the coals shimmered.

"I wonder how far it is to their site," Jane said.

"It must be the one on the point we passed, with the three tents."

Jane checked that the tent zipper was closed. The bugs weren't bad, but just in case. Tugged on the fly to make sure it was secure. It didn't look like rain, but storms came out of nowhere up here.

Did you not say to Rachel, let's go check out some dads?

She found her own Petzl in her backpack, pressed the button four times, testing the beams: strong, medium, soft, then flashing. Settled on strong. Rachel adjusted hers and they entered the black space in the brush. Holding the silent walkie-talkie. Rufy leaping over low bushes beside them on the path, staying close.

Jane pictured miners heading into a coal shaft listening for the canary, tripping through the dark tunnel. Rachel ahead of her, parting the trees with her hands, holding back branches so they wouldn't hit Jane in the face. Jane thought she looked like a lovely folk dancer accommodating partners left and right.

You're an experienced camper. You know the dangers.

She tilted her head farther up the path, the Petzl illuminating still more trees.

The park is known for its black bears. Did you not know that a black bear defends itself if surprised? Do you still think it's appropriate for a boy to play with a spear?

She chose to picture the end of the path, the trees becoming thinner, the heartbeat of light finally coming into view. The tight circle of rosy male faces welcoming them. As if it were just another night up north, nothing discovered or revealed. The kind of campfire with beer and feet up and ribald jokes, the occasional chorus of a familiar Top Ten song. Tales of embarrassing moments, softened in the telling. The shifting of bodies on a log, the circle expanding to let the two of them in. The yellow bird that went before them perched on a campstool, singing. And Jane whispering, "We thought we'd lost you."

SCRATCH

1.

In her final year at York University, Beth became obsessed with the washroom graffiti on campus. She loved the private conversations, the political discourse. The different colours of pen and large angry letters. Sometimes it began with something like *Men don't protect women anymore.* Then a series of responses. Often daily. A story in progress. Punctuated with *fuck* or *bitch* or *dyke.* Inevitably the dialogue ran out of space or patience or deteriorated into a rant. She loved that each washroom seemed to have a genre. Politics. Sex. Irony everywhere. She loved that the caretakers rarely washed the walls.

Beth began to read theories about graffiti. From the

Italian *graffiare*: to scratch. Latin accounts of disease and natural disaster etched onto the saints of chapels. *Elles font corps avec*: becoming one with the body of the saint. The ritual of graffiti: a way of imposing structure and meaning on disruptive events. Urban graffiti: a claiming of public space, art beyond gallery walls. The markings of gang territory, underground forces made visible. Shopkeepers and business owners trying to gain back power through scrubbing and whitewashing.

She wanted to do her psychology thesis on the differences between male and female graffiti. She needed to control the variables. She collected samples from high school washrooms because the age range was defined. College washrooms were frequented by too broad a population sample.

She didn't have a boyfriend at the time, so she asked her father to accompany her.

"Why are you interested in filth?" But he reluctantly agreed. "No daughter of mine is sneaking into boys' rooms."

They lingered in the hallways during night school, pretending to be students, ducking in and out of washrooms until a teacher or principal got suspicious. After several unsuccessful visits to Victoria Park S.S., Wexford Collegiate, and David and Mary Thomson C.I., she thought the students must be either too scared to write on toilet walls or too polite. Then she realized the caretakers had a hand in this. At the end of each day the stalls were scrubbed clean. Occasionally faint traces of history could be seen, but the caretakers removed any marks.

She hit the jackpot with Earl Haig Secondary School, twice as large as the others. The caretakers hadn't finished their rounds. In the girls' room: hearts, hearts, and more hearts. *I love Ray. Ray loves me.* Names like math equations: *Leslie + John. Sherri + Steven.* Each piece of graffiti was copied onto a recipe card, to be sorted later on her bedroom floor.

Her father was smiling too when he came out of the boys' room. He handed over his recipe cards reluctantly. In the centre of each was a faint, hurried sketch of a penis, as if he'd been afraid to make the commitment. Some vertical. Some horizontal. With and without balls. And lots of imperatives. *Fuck you. Fuck her.* Or just *Fuck.*

"This is great," she said.

He tried to scowl. "By the way, they're drawn to scale."

2.

When Beth became a high school art teacher, she had her students design murals, projecting their creations onto various walls around the school and filling them in with latex paint. They spilled a lot, clogging the sinks in the art room. She knew she was making an enemy of Nick, the caretaker, so she spent much of her prep time running around the hallways with a sponge, becoming highly adept at spotting latex drips that were not part of the floor design. The students' pride in their work outweighed Beth's stress.

Her favourite mural was outside the art room. She could see it from her desk. Since the beginning of time there had been a grey garbage bin in front of that wall. Now there was a rainbow spilling from an upside-down paint can. Beth had simply moved the bin across the hall. But when the work was finally complete, the garbage can reappeared in front of it. An oversight, she thought. She moved it back and told Nick this was now a wall of art. He nodded. The chiselled lines around his mouth, from summers spent in Greece, tightened into a conciliatory smile. But the next morning the can was blocking the painting.

One night Beth was working late and overheard Nick speaking to Barb next door: "Every night she move it over and every night I move it back. Ha!" Each morning she felt her stomach tighten on the drive to work, thinking of the moment when she would turn the corner into the upstairs hallway. Every time she saw the bin in front of the mural her day was ruined.

She tried going to the principal. "Why don't you paint it? Make it part of the mural?" He was building a collaborative school culture. He asked her to come to some consensus with Nick. She told him, half jokingly, that if he found the bin in the Dumpster one day, he couldn't blame her. For the rest of the year Beth fought this battle.

She began dreaming of going away. Ordered adventure travel pamphlets, obsessively studying pictures from the other side of the world: jungles, mountains, deserts. She finally chose Thailand for her summer vacation, the farthest possible place from Markham High.

3.

She stayed in a forest monastery at Suan Mokh. A ten-day silent retreat with seventy other travellers. She slept on a concrete platform with a straw mat to protect her from the scorpions and a mosquito net to keep out the malaria. Her clothes were whittled down to a few sarongs and shirts, the rest of her possessions and books stored in a locker. She was given a candle for her 5 a.m. wake-up and teeth-brushing under the stars. Walking, sitting, standing: six hours of meditation punctuated by breakfast and lunch. Coconuts fell like bombs; one was rumoured to have killed a girl from Iowa. Beth was supposed to contemplate the life cycle of the lotus in the pond, the water trundling along the river. The certainty of change. But all she could do was think about her growing knee pain, endure the torture of sleepiness during meditation, promise to eat less rice at the next meal.

Twice a day Beth washed her sweat-soaked clothes in a vat of green water. Showers involved a bowl dipped and scooped over her sarong-covered body, soap lathered through the bright cloth. Then caffeine-free tea and a banana for dinner before the evening lecture on dharma and the benefits of non-attachment. It was here that she learned she did not exist. The self was really an aggregate of the five senses. And to attach to a self was to suffer. To desire was to suffer. If she sat long enough with anger, it would transform into compassion. She must follow the breath. Shake off thoughts of the tofu and greens that would fill her breakfast bowl. Ignore the mosquito landing on her forehead. Forego chemicals like insecticides so that all creatures could live. Including the red ants building a monastery of their own in the squat toilet. Chase the breath, like a tiger. Ignore the itchy red blotches on her ass from late-night squats.

On day eight they were told, if they wished, they could break their vow of silence to ask the head monk a question in private. The only sound Beth had uttered was the scream she'd let out the night a snake crawled into the women's dorm. She was nervous but she knew she needed to talk with the monk.

He was sitting on a bamboo platform, legs folded beneath his orange robe, hot tea being served to him by one of the teachers. He sat looking off into the distance.

She fitted herself into half-lotus, the best her legs could do. He turned to her then, placed his hands together in front of his chest, and said, "*Sawadee krap.*" His pointed cheekbones unmoving beneath his thin brown skin, wrinkles fine as cat whiskers.

"I want to tell you a story," Beth said. And she told him about the caretaker and the garbage can and the murals on the wall, the daily game of art versus garbage. She tried to disguise the power struggle. Surely she had a responsibility to protect her students' expression? To be their advocate? To fight the lesser ideals of the caretaker?

The question she asked the monk was, "Should I be angry?"

He looked at her and said, "You are the mother of many children, yet every morning you have angry face." And he looked away, towards the world beyond the monastery walls, lethal coconuts, snakes and scorpions.

On the final day of the retreat, the monks broke them into small gender-specific discussion groups and asked them to choose a spokesperson to summarize their experience. They set up a microphone by candlelight in the meditation hall. Beth and the others sat cross-legged on their straw mats in the centre. The orange robes were relegated to the periphery. For the first time in ten days, the monks were the listeners. Beth spoke for her group, saying that many of them had cried, let go of old hurts, visualized a release, experienced compassion and new-found understanding.

Then the men shared. One of the speakers looked like a gum-chewing, TV-watching westerner. He wore a San Francisco baseball cap. Beth had pegged him early in the week as newly attached to the redhead on the far side of the meditation hall. For the first few days she'd watched them from her cushion at the back. The couple smiled often at one another. By day three, though, they were glancing at each other less. The man was clearly having trouble concentrating during the half-hour sit. He had grown more agitated, doing vigorous sit-ups in the courtyard every day after breakfast.

When he took the microphone, he said there was only one thing he and the guys had thought about: sex. He grinned. The power of saying it in front of the monks, who were laughing along with all the other graduates. The angry, tense face Beth had watched all week had been wiped clean. Probably not due to hours spent contemplating compassion. Probably due to a reunion with the redhead. And knowing he would never choose to endure such self-exploration again.

4.

Beth was the only one in her psychology thesis class who found statistically significant results. She sorted the recipe cards on her bedroom floor. Stared at piles of male markings and words: *nigger, motherfucker.* She concluded male graffiti was more sexual, racist, and aggressive than female graffiti. Of course she had to quantify those words. In which pile did *fuck* belong? If it had *go* in front of it or *you* after it, or an exclamation mark — *Fuck!* — it could be categorized as aggressive. But *fuck* on its own could be just a thought. A quiet meditation on the act. Or a request. A word sent out like karma, hoping it would come back like a boomerang. The size of the letters, the boldness, the use of uppercase, all helped her classify. She began to see how handwriting experts had to be almost psychic. She began to form pictures of young men in stalls trying to gain a sense of control. *Fuck you.*

Beth studied the pile of hearts from the girls' washrooms. Why only one type of drawing? A universal symbol. No breasts. No vaginas. Those Beth saw in university washrooms, but here in the high schools it was hearts. The longer she stared at them the more she saw them as two question marks, one forwards, one backwards. Sometimes there was a question mark in the equation: *Louise + ?* While the boys were identifying with a giant phallus, the girls were asking, *Who loves me?*

She titled her thesis "Hearts vs. Penises."

5 ·

When Beth came home from Thailand, she returned to her art job at Markham High. In late August she began making the long morning drive to work to get the room ready for September. She kept her hands loose on the wheel, practised her breathing, monitored her belly for tension. None. The building was quiet, empty. She climbed the stairs to the upper hallway, inhaling white light, and when she rounded the corner, she could see the garbage can standing in front of the mural. Nick was sweeping the floor near the drinking fountain, his back to her. She chased her breath like a great tiger with silk paws, and floated down the corridor towards him.

TEXAS

I've finally figured it out — in Texas, of all places. Slow is sexy. I always thought you had to cram it all in, like a résumé. Give each new man mile-a-minute anecdotes, *That's me, leaping before I look,* hands like an apprentice magician, transforming my napkin into a perky lotus, voila.

This is why I never hooked a guy. Why I'm forty-three and in a trailer park in Brownsville, Texas, spending my vacation with my parents.

The trailer's as expected: floral couch, floral cushions, floral curtains. Two-year-old *Reader's Digest*s on the shin-barking coffee table. A fuzzy fuchsia disc clutching the simulated wood toilet seat. Cupboards packed with Melmac plates, the kind you can't break in a domestic dispute. My parents have moved out of the bedroom — the one with just enough space to walk around the bed — and are sleeping in an L on the living/dining room benches so I'll be comfortable and will want to join them again next winter. The place is not really their style, even though it's got a carport, a covered veranda. You can't disguise a shipwrecked dinghy on a slab of concrete.

"Take the golf cart anytime." As if I've just got my licence and they're looking for reasons to keep me from applying to university abroad.

The cart goes fifteen kilometres an hour. Roads wind around the gated complex, the rear eyes of trailers facing eighteen holes of rolling green. The eighth hole not ten feet from my bedroom window with the curtains that collapse, rod and all, onto the bed each time I try to open them. I sit on the patio, just big enough for a tap dance. Golf carts pull up as regular as a carnival ride. Each with a lone female driver, golf bag like a husband in the passenger seat. No cartpooling here. The ladies swing their legs sideways, lever their bellies out two steps. Backhand a five-iron like an arrow out of a quiver and whack the ball without so much as a practice swing. Counting on par 120, the number of minutes to kill before lunch.

I take the cart out on the road that leads to the swimming pool. The road with the speed bumps. Past the Mexicans riding lawnmowers like put-out-to-pasture horses. It's as if I'm suddenly in a parade, heads automatically rising from newspapers, the hospitable hand-wave from each deckchair. The American flags, wooden birds with open mouths nailed to mailboxes, scarecrows with one leg out. *This is as good as Oz.* No matter how they dress each trailer, I see a de-winged bug sleeping to forget what's lost. Even the deluxe models that make my dad say, "Maybe next year."

I spend the week worrying that lethargy will show up on my thighs. The long drives to strip malls, bypassing Mexican corner shops with *everything cheaper*, but Mom says, "You never really know what you're getting." Besides, Walmart has everything. Everything but a man.

I'm withering in Texas.

My parents have come here to hang out with the Brysons, who spend most of the week ignoring them, preferring their bridge-playing friends. The Brysons are renting the trailer next to the lady who trains black Labs for the blind. It's slow enough here; there's lots of time for mistakes, time to figure things out.

Our one outing with the Brysons. Jed sits in front with Dad to navigate without a map. Shelly smushes in with Mom and me so we're shoulder-locked. When we get to Pete's Fluttering Wings Bird 'n' Butterfly Ranch, I walk really slowly, practising to get a man. I stare through the mesh screens. Budgies, blue and green, pretend they won't fly given an open door. We watch an eight-millimetre film: *Spread Your Wings*. Then walk through a row of tiny trees trapped in hairnet mesh. Hundreds of cocoons like burned-out Christmas tree lights. I'm walking down the aisle thinking *harvest*. Trying not to see it as sinister.

It seems odd to find something so minute as a cocoon in Texas. Here among the long stretches of road, the warehouse restaurants, the big-bodied couples forever married, quietly masticating brisket that hangs off their plates. The huge parking lots with yellow runway lines, the long queue

to buy grapefruit. The hour-long drive to an empty movie
theatre big as a bowling alley. The screen showing an old
pickup truck crossing the Mexico/U.S. border. Brown bodies packed beneath a tarp in the back, eyes closed in prayer.

Excruciating boredom, every-moment questioning of my
life, drives me to aquafit in the morning. I am the only
one in the pool until two minutes to nine. Except for the
Mexican with the net, mechanically skimming the already
clean surface. The ladies come with their breasts harnessed
in underwire, bathing suit bottoms smacking with purple
and pink flowers. They're each hugging a basketball and
holding a plywood ring. Somebody's husband's been busy.
They place their balls in the homemade holders, a line of
Saturns by the side of the pool. Then dip their veined legs
in the grey water, look up at the sky. "Storm again today."
    The storm that never came yesterday. Or the day before.
    I can tell the aquafit instructor's in a rut too. She's as
young as me. She pushes a button on her mini tape deck
and starts punching. *Muhammad Ali, one-two, one-two.
Now cycle to Africa, one-two-three, one-two-three.* The
loud ladies with their drawls. "Gladys will be away all
week. Cancer." Like it's a vacation. There's an old man who
looks like Santa lowering himself from his wheelchair into
the shallow end.
    "Circle arms, dear," the ladies say to me mid-gossip.
I'm trying to see what they're doing while keeping an eye
on Santa. He's moving through the water now — slowly,
but he's moving. "My god, it's like I'm walking." There's
a miracle in the shallow end and they're talking about

Slimfast. "Twelve dollars a day but the portions leave you wanting."

My father spends the week doing a thousand-piece puzzle of white and powder-pink flowers. Angry with the Brysons. Finally, on St. Patrick's Day, they accept my parents' invite. Mom buys a piece of bristol board and a green Magic Marker. The shamrock looks like the four-leaf clover I spent backyard summers scouring for. "Keep looking," Mom always said. She hangs the poster in the carport so the Brysons will know there's something to celebrate.

Their eldest son, Wayne, comes with his two boys. Fresh from the divorce. I always had a crush on him but he had googly eyes for my sister's big boobs and skinny bum. He asked her to go to the grade nine dance. Spent most of the night with his friends in the washroom, downing Southern Comfort. He made his sloppy move in the park on the walk home. They kind of tumbled around in the grass and didn't realize until they stood up that he'd rolled in dog poo. That was the end of it for her.

Everyone puts on a few pounds, a few wrinkles, but I've held steady. I can see Wayne's pleasant surprise, giving me the up-down. I'm doubly nice to his kids, trying to play "Happy Birthday" on the mini-accordion I bought in Mexico. Just over the Rio Grande border running through our security-patrolled park. Every day twenty get caught swimming to America.

Luckily I've put on my shorts, and Mom's said, "You look nice." I think Wayne's staying for a week. "Maybe we could play golf," I say. But I spend the rest of my vacation sharing my parents' lament, *Why don't they call?*

‹ ‹ ‹

I'm deciphering pinks. Pale's the hardest because it's sixty percent of the puzzle. I give it my best shot, choose the dark pieces first. Hold each like a fake fingernail, Bargirl Red, hovering over gaping holes. I keep consulting the bigger picture, trying to remember what I'm here for.

Some sun, some slow.

But when I see pale is all that's left, I think of those Mexicans sitting in the river. Waiting for a miracle. Throughout the night, holstered sheriffs pass over them again and again. Spotlights graze their wet hair. So many men, waiting to be picked.

THIXATROPIC

"Thixatropic," Heather says, as if it's an interesting word. As if Nadine should scribble it down in her notebook.

"Oooh." A squeal from the back of the "studio," which, it turns out, is a roadside industrial garage near King City.

Nadine's paying big bucks for the week-long course. "What's that?" she asks.

Heather has a man body with breasts. Her shoulders are well-defined softballs, arms hanging straight down. A beginning sculptor's first, failed piece. Her golden curls are youthful but her face has obviously never worn sunscreen.

"It describes the property of certain mixtures that become temporarily fluid when shaken or stirred then revert back to the gel state." Heather scans the ground as she talks, never looking into the eyes of the dozen students surrounding the chart on a stand. Nadine's not like the others. These people are her parents' age.

"What the hell?" Nadine whispers to John, with his past-expiration corduroys. She tolerates him in case she needs to remember the ratio of cement to aggregate. The rest, with their polyester pants and floral appliqué sweatshirts, she dismisses. Housewives and hobbyists, empty-nesters exploring their sublimated creativity in the form of garden ornaments.

Although Heather appears oaf-like, her hearing is that of a wolf. "It means if you keep touching it and going over it, it loses what holds it together," she says loudly, moving to the workbench in front of the open garage door. The group follows her, geese with notebooks. She grabs the cutters with her bulbous fingers, tilts a roll of chicken wire towards her like a dance partner, unrolling it quickly. A few snips and there's a piece of mesh on the workbench like a wrestled fish. Her head tilts forward as if spilling an idea.

"I've been thinking about a reclining lion." She's bending the screen without effort. A head appears, then a big belly.

She darts over to the chart stand, the group following. She hovers an inch away from it like she's reading Braille. Talks to the paper for ten minutes while they all lean in to catch what *air-entraining admixture* is. When she goes to reach for the eight-ounce container of Concrete Bond, her arm lifts only as high as her conical breasts, barely covered by a well-worn muscle shirt.

"Could you get that for me?" she asks no one in particular.

"She's just had both hips replaced," John whispers, clutching his birdbath sketches. "She's on a waiting list for her shoulders."

Nadine chooses a workspace next to John. Sits on her stool, looking at her sketches of a laughing Buddha. He's not the slim one she saw in countless Tibetan monasteries. He's more Chinese. She wants the symbolism of abundance, contentment. She's added gestures of enlightenment. His left hand lying in his lap, palm upward. His right wrist bending over the right knee, fingers slightly touching the earth, transforming anger into wisdom.

Everyone in the studio is working with conviction. Making armatures from cardboard or soft foam, mummy-wrapping with mesh. Using a large cooking spoon or trowel to embed cement mix in the wire until it protrudes a quarter-inch through the other side. Smoothing it like cake icing with a damp sponge. They squint like Picasso, compare their pieces with magazine pictures, plastic-wrapped photos. Perhaps their families have commissioned them. A butterfly-shaped stool for the patio. One Doric column to hold the chrysanthemum by the front door.

Nadine knows she should be less cynical. Has nothing stayed with her from her trip? Since her ten-month tour through Tibet, she's begun sleeping a lot, not wanting to get out of bed. Her parents said, "Come stay with us." When she arrived in King City, her mother handed her the brochure: "Art for Pleasure." She began feeding Nadine salmon every day in order to build up her serotonin levels, a trick she'd read about in *Potatoes Not Prozac*.

In Tibet Nadine had watched temple-goers move clockwise, skimming monastery walls with yak-buttered fingers. Uneven stone sticky with coins and bills. Each nomad with his bag of butter like fun-fair popcorn, spooned into brass bowls, a dozen tiny flames. Hands together in front of their chests, they bowed to burgundy-robed monks. Wrapped white scarves around framed photos of smiling lamas. In her journal she obsessively drew the recurring barley-and-wheat-dough sculptures found on altars. *Torma*, she wrote, not knowing their significance. Two round spheres, one atop the other like a tiny snowman, sometimes dipped in red. What did they mean? Norbu, the van driver, explained: "Mind and body. Joined through the breath."

She tries wrapping a piece of mesh into two balls but it keeps cutting her hands. She isn't sure how to join them because Heather hasn't clearly explained. John lends her an extra pair of gloves. He shows her how to cut the galvanized reinforcing rods into short lengths and bend them with a hammer and a bench vise. Then he teaches her how to fix them together with soft black iron tie wire, twisting the ends together to make a pigtail.

Nadine breathes. She breathes in her memory of juniper incense. The slow, purposeful movements of monks. Where is the peace she vowed to bring home? Within one month of being in Toronto she felt it slipping through her fingers, like the ragged prayer flags at high passes on the plateau, flapping into disintegration. By the end of the day she has a skeleton the size of a small child, covered in a thin layer of patchy cement.

On Tuesday Nadine arrives early at the studio. It takes a moment before she realizes that Heather is among the still grey figures. She's sitting on a stool next to the workbench nearest the door, wearing the same clothes as yesterday. When she sees Nadine, she starts fiddling with the tools on her workbench, keeping her head down. Nadine says good morning twice before Heather looks up and nods.

Someone has covered her Buddha with a blue tarp. She remembers now that she's supposed to keep it semi-moist. She doesn't remove the tarp. She sits so it blocks her view of Heather and watches as the other students arrive and begin laying out their tools. Lesley starts up the concrete mixer in the parking lot, Jack shovels a pile of gravel into the open-mouth drum.

Heather gives a quick lecture on sanding the layer of dried cement. Nadine is nowhere near this stage. Others scrape, carve ornate flowers, chisel fish scales and attach limbs while the concrete is still malleable, still "green," as Heather says. Nadine goes out to where Brenda is watching the mixer drum rotate, waiting for it to be the right consistency. She's been having trouble keeping her life-size gardener upright.

"She's given us no real instruction," Nadine says.

"Hmm," Brenda mumbles. What's wrong with these people? Nadine thinks.

Nadine works all morning putting ears on her Buddha. They keep sliding down the side of his neck. She decides he will be Deaf Buddha, and goes for a stroll around the studio. With her bowl-cut hair, Pat is as manly as her miniature Winston Churchill. Hands on his hips, cigar clenched in perfectly square teeth. "How did you know how to make his arms stay?"

"I just played with it till I figured it out."

"She never says good morning, never makes eye contact," Nadine says to Jack, who is fixing the hands of a Big Ben tower, half past twelve.

"That's the time of my son Ben's birth."

Nadine whines to Lesley, who is now making a concrete

inukshuk, although the parking lot is full of rectangular rocks. "She's spoken to me once. She doesn't even know what I'm working on."

When Lesley gives her no satisfaction, Nadine returns to her piece. She spends the day adding layers, making double, triple chins to deepen Buddha's joy, but the concrete keeps slipping onto his chest.

Suddenly Heather is standing behind her. "You should have used expanded steel instead of chicken wire, or at least added layers until the openings were a half-inch across," she says.

"I just wanted to make a small Buddha for my apartment. But I keep slapping more layers of cement on. I don't really know what I'm doing."

With her man hand, Heather removes the jowls and chins. In one swoop he's a skinny, retentive Thai Buddha, not at all the life-guzzling Buddha Nadine had planned.

Heather moves on to John, Nadine holding back the tears. The sketches of Buddha on her bench start to blur. She walks quickly out of the garage, plastic bag in hand, heading for the mixer at the edge of the lot.

She stops to look at the blue sky, remembering the crisp, frigid days on the plateau, always a blue sky. A monk doesn't cry. She didn't cry once on her trip, bathing in frozen rivers, crossing tough terrain in a Jeep with busted shock absorbers, battling carsickness, altitude sickness.

When she reaches the mixer, Heather is already there, scooping wet cement into a Loblaws bag. Nadine holds open her plastic sack. Heather turns to her and says, "Oh, there's none left," and walks away. Nadine stares into the cylinder, the bits of leftover rubble.

On Wednesday Nadine comes a half-hour late, finds

everyone working happily. John's now building a reproduction of a Notre Dame gargoyle ready to pounce. Then she sees her Buddha's head, slumped forward on his chest.

"His forehead was too large. Too much thinking." John snickers.

"What?"

"You'll have to put in a stake."

"You mean right through him? How am I going to do that?"

"How should I know?"

That's it, Nadine thinks. She weaves her way through the workbenches and aproned artists stepping back to admire their work, careful not to bump a mermaid's tail or topple a three-tiered fountain. Strides to the end of the lot, hops in her parents' Volvo, and drives like a madwoman into town, to the administrative office of Art for Pleasure.

Zoe, the program head, invites her to sit in her cramped office, where a wooden doll stands skewered by a steel rod on her desk, one hand raised to its ear as though it's eavesdropping. Zoe is a short woman with hair that's been encouraged to follow its own creative path. She's staring at Nadine's face as if she's analyzing a painting, looking for focal points: Nadine's red eyes, her quivering lip.

"For two days now she's been working on her lion with its paw in the air. It's lovely. You should see it," Nadine says sarcastically.

Zoe nods sympathetically.

"I know she's some well-known sculptor or something." She's trying to get the words out through sobs now. "But I'm not learning a thing."

Zoe tells Nadine to take a breath.

"Would you like us to put you in another course?"

"No, I just want to take my Buddha and go home."

"Leave this with me."

"I don't want her to know I said anything. I'm not one to complain. Do you have a Kleenex?"

Zoe hands her the box. "Just leave this with me."

Nadine stops for lunch at a diner in town. Opts for a double burger with chunky fries when she can't find salmon on the menu. By the time she returns, Zoe is in the warehouse circulating amongst the students, taking a subtle poll on what they think of the instructor. Nadine knows the importance of word of mouth, feels certain Heather won't be asked back.

Nadine watches Zoe, in sandals and a gypsy skirt, face to chest with Heather outside. Heather stands still as Michelangelo's *David*, cement mix calcifying on her limp forearms. Then her steel-toed work boot swipes the gravel twice, like a dog's hind leg after a pee.

That afternoon Heather teaches a final lesson on repairing broken appendages, applying acrylic latex stains and Thompson's WaterSeal. She's preparing them for the future, when their figures will live outside, exposed to the elements. She stands to the side of the chart easel so they can see, circulates around the room three or four times.

When she gets to Nadine's figure, she scrapes away the back of his cracking neck. She inserts a strip of precut metal, like a six-inch ruler, and uses the black tie wire to fasten it to the underlying armature. Then she makes tiny discs of concrete, fitting them in place with surgeon-like precision.

"Make each patty thin, like a McDonald's burger," Heather advises her before she moves on to the next student.

Now that the head is upright, Buddha's ears appear long and droopy. Nadine remembers this signifies wisdom. They sit on his shoulders, on either side of a chin that is now perfect. She finds the patience to embed the mesh slowly.

Nadine knows that wet concrete is strongest, so she mists it every twenty minutes. She takes a break, wraps it in drenched paper towels. When she comes back, Buddha is sweating. She knows things are moving forward, working themselves out.

She plugs away with renewed vigour and hope. Imagining the aggregates interlocking, picturing the sharp, irregular crystals that Heather drew in thick black Magic Marker on the chart paper, saying, "They grow, they *actually* grow," as if it's the most exciting discovery of modern science. Now Nadine feels excitement too. She doesn't play with the chin anymore. She wants to prevent future cracking, to ensure tensile strength.

On Thursday Nadine uses a plastic knife to chisel the long, graceful fingers resting on Buddha's knee. She gives shape to the puffy eyelids, the pupils in a meditative downward gaze. She deepens the grooves of his sleeves so they gather like silk in the crooks of his elbows. She shapes his fingernails and draws a steady lifeline in his upturned palm. He is as fine now as the other sculptures in the warehouse: the Easter Island monolith, the dragon with ribbed wings, the life-size sunbather with her floppy hat. He is exactly what she wanted.

On Friday Heather asks John to assist Nadine. They lift the once-intended coffee-table Buddha onto the scale to calculate how much she owes for materials: 110 pounds.

Heather and Nadine slide him into the back of her parents'

—

sedan, facing out. Nadine wraps a picnic blanket around his shoulders while Heather places a piece of cardboard between his forehead and the glass. Then Heather stands erect, making eye contact with her for the first time.

"Thanks for everything," Nadine hears herself mumbling. Something passes through Heather's eyes, as if she's just gleaned a punchline.

Nadine drives below the speed limit to her parents' garden. There's comfort in knowing she's added the entraining agent, intentionally creating microscopic air bubbles. That she's given him durability, especially in winter, during the freezes and the thaws. She leaves him under a small pine tree, trimming the lowest branches so she can admire his humble, compassionate profile, before heading home to the city.

THE EXCHANGE

Diana wasn't sure how she felt about the fifth floor of
the newly renovated Art Gallery of Ontario. The high-
ceilinged room housed three totem poles made from
hockey bags. She tilted her head up to take in their
spiritual grandeur. She didn't quite get the hockey bags.
A reference to her ancestors' mistreatment of Natives, she
assumed, and accepted the responsibility, breathed in the
shame, silently asked for forgiveness.

She caught sight of Henry for the first time through
the space between the poles. His white hair thick, full, in
defiance of his age. He was stepping close to the sculpture,
peering at the details. Beak-nose pouches, flat black eyes,
square red chins, huge zipper lips.

They were the only two in the room. She scrambled to

think of some clever remark. "This reminds me of a piece in Kleinburg," she might say. She'd seen a tepee made of baseball bats and bases at the McMichael gallery. Wondered if it was by the same artist. She could say, "This is his best work to date."

She hesitated to call herself an artist; she was self-taught. *Naive*, the word often used to describe folk artists like her. She took the description as permission. She painted cows and chickens, completely devoid of history. She'd never had her own show. The trip to the AGO was part of her resolution to gather some vocabulary. With each piece she's looked at the card on the wall, saying the artist's name aloud twice, imprinting it aurally into memory.

She didn't want the man to see her check the museum label before making her thoughtful comment, so she moved nearer to him, pretending to join him in studying the way the seams were joined.

"This would look good on my property." He didn't look at her when he spoke. But Diana had enough to go on. The word *property*, and the way he'd interpreted her move towards him as opportunity. She looked at the black scarf wrapped twice around his neck, his full-length black wool coat, fully done up, as if he'd just stopped by for a quick fill-up. Only his leather gloves had been removed. The fingers stuck out from his grasp, two hands trying to escape.

She looked at his eyes, the wrinkles of a man whose life is just beginning to leave an impression. She couldn't tell if he was single. The slight puddle forming around his black rubbers, the expensive shoes beneath, the way he seemed firmly planted there, suggested long-time marriage. Perhaps newly broken up, desperate for solace, using the gallery the way some men sit in the pews of a downtown church on their lunch hour.

"This needs a lot of space to breathe. You must have a large property." There — spiritual, subtle.

"I do. I will. It's still in the planning stages."

"Hockey bags, right?" Fishing.

"Looks like it. I'm not much of a fan."

Perfect, she thought.

"This one here. Have you seen this?" He gestured behind him. A large glass display case, an architectural model of a sprawling city, including cathedrals and monuments that looked vaguely familiar to her.

"'Number 42: San Marco Square, Venice.' Where's forty-two? . . . Oh, it's a wolf. Hmmm. What's this about?" Recruit him as expert.

"I think it's a statement on global urban planning, the displacement of wild inhabitants."

Diana stood looking at the roads and trees, wondering how the artist had conceived of such a project.

"It reminds me of my architectural plans," he went on. "I'm rebuilding a farmhouse up north, over a hundred years old. Working with the engineers to get it just right. We're gutting the insides." *We.*

"Your family must be excited."

"They are." *Shoot. No further ahead. Should have said "your wife."*

"The kids get to design their bedrooms."

Diana had the urge to fall into her usual role of questioner, rendering herself invisible. Most men didn't notice. But Dr. Creemore had told her these were the wrong men. *Crymore. Seemore.* Two nicknames she used to describe her therapist, depending on the session. She now knew she had to stop waiting for them to ask her things, had to take up space from the beginning.

She turned away from him. Towards the video projection on the wall. It was a slow zoom-out, a field of snow, the tops of three pine trees slowly coming into view.

He followed, as hoped. Stood next to her. She felt like she had the one time she'd made a bold move while playing pool and found she'd actually visualized where the white ball would end up.

"I love this," she said.

He stared at her face as if looking at hockey-bag seams. Smiled so that she could see his teeth were bleached. Each tooth a keystone to her well-being.

The camera continued to reveal more snow. The pulling back calmed her, settled her need to fill the space with chatter, to put him at ease. He stood close to her, perhaps to get the best vantage point on the piece, but she interpreted it as a sign. The space between them familiar. The camera took several minutes, panning out to a bird's-eye view of a huge field. All the while she pictured his property. Looking out from his farmhouse window, beside a four-poster smothered in handmade quilts. Finally a clearing in the snow appeared. A square of ice, several people skating. Perhaps a family.

"My ex hates snow." Present tense. But at least he'd offered *ex*.

‹ ‹ ‹

He walked her through the skeleton of the house, pointing to the emptiness. That will be Zack's room. That one's

Martha's. The family room. His big hands swirled like a conjuror's amidst the pine beams and square window frames. She could see the distant lake, the hills. Diana pictured herself in the scene, rescued from the city, where her cows and chickens continually got lost. She saw her booth at a small-town art fair, the kind run by wise post-menses women, their tousled, wiry hair worn long. Trading business cards and eating whole-grain lunches out of Tupperware containers. Customers milling about, offering compliments; even the occasional sale.

They stood in the second-floor master bedroom, a gaping hole where the Juliet balcony would be. A curtain of thick plastic open at the bottom, flapping in the wind, inviting lovelorn leaps. He led her into a completely tiled room where two flat showerheads hung like surveillance mikes. Placing her under one, he stood under the other. He lifted one arm up, pretended to rub suds into his armpit. He moved both his hands to his chest, rotated them around his shirt pockets like a novice stripper. His body tight and erect as a top-selling wrench. His father had just died, making him president of the Trinz Tool Company. The money striking her then. The way a cowhide or a rooster comb shimmered with possibility.

‹ ‹ ‹

The drywall compound was still wet when she moved in with her boxy canvases and her suitcase full of acrylics like so many squished toothpaste tubes. Her brushes she arranged in jars along the windowsill like drying flowers. He started work right away on plans for a studio next to the house. They needed room for all the art he wanted to buy. He could finally be a collector.

His well-rounded kids visited every other week. Two boys, two girls, all two years apart. The eldest fourteen, with no sign yet of pubescent rebellion. He plugged them into a complicated schedule of cultural and social education. Dinners consisted of didactic talks, lessons learned in business. Weekends were filled with museums, galleries, tennis lessons, choir practice, play rehearsals. They awoke early for school, often before Diana, and she watched their backpacks disappearing into the SUV, waved goodbye to the tinted windows.

It was all part of the deal. Her brand-new studio, her new country life, the invitation to be a big fish in a small pond. She joined the Church Quilters, a group of retired women who walked three miles before breakfast and never missed the Tuesday meeting. She joined them in the room above the antique shop, around the taut square cloth, awed by their capacity for gossip. Their hands on autopilot. Sewing intricate patterns with names: Oh My Stars, Winding Ways, Almost a Flower Garden.

They picked her up like a dropped stitch. "I hear Henry's building you a castle, complete with moat and drawbridge," one said with a wink. Others chiming in with "Uh-huh" and "Oh, really?" and "My George is like that." She began to talk and talk.

"Henry's always got something in the works. We've got a vegetable garden the size of an Olympic pool. And the wildflowers. He's planted them according to colour. The same order as in the spectrum, so we'll have a rainbow in the spring. We've got a path made out of rocks he found down the back of the property. He drew it out first, how they'd all fit together. It leads to the stump garden."

"What on earth?"

"You've heard of a Zen garden? You can just go and look at them, the way the Japanese sit and look at rocks."

By the time she'd looked up from her sewing, the other quilters' hands had paused. Their eyes glistened with secrets. She didn't say anything more.

The kitchen was the last room to be finished. Appliances new, shiny silver, so Diana could watch the Diana who prepared meals. The freezer at the bottom of the fridge, a warmer at the foot of the oven, two microwaves, all built-ins. She spent the first month opening the wrong doors. Some days Henry hovered — the garlic wasn't minced finely enough, the sandwiches were to be cut on the diagonal, tomatoes quartered, not sliced.

"I thought I told you to use the cutting-board papers." He pointed to a scratch in the wood. "There's no such thing as a mistake."

She got into the habit of slipping a protector on like a condom before choosing one of fourteen knives asleep in the holder.

‹ ‹ ‹

Henry acquired art on business trips. His collection grew; soon every inch of the living room displayed paintings of rural villages, maritime towns, farmers in fields. One day Henry said, "I've fallen in love with a woman in the gallery." He went out to the car and brought her inside, hung her on the kitchen wall. "You'll love her too."

It wasn't folksy, like the rest. It was *fine art*. Three life-size women were seated at a wooden dining table like theirs. Or one woman painted three times. An anniversary gift, Henry said.

"They're all the same," Diana said.

Henry smiled knowingly. "It's called *The Exchange*."

The figure on the right appeared to be speaking, her elbows on the table, hands in the air, gesticulating. The middle one looked towards the one on the right, but her eyes showed she was thinking about other things. The one on the left had oriented her body towards the other two, but her face looked directly out at Henry and Diana. As if to say, *One year, eh?*

"It's very compelling," Diana said. "You can't even see the brushstrokes."

"I knew you'd love it."

She noticed that Henry looked at the woman in the painting often. Sometimes standing directly in front of the repeated figure, his face beaming with lust. His gaze travelling over the model's body. All three versions wore the same plum-coloured sundress, revealing bare arms, cream-coloured shoulders, a line of cleavage. The signature, *Costa*, contoured the calf. There was a point where the flowered tablecloth hung as if falling over buttocks, collecting in the crack. His eyes traversed this spot like a canoeist through a tricky place in a river.

One day, not long after *The Exchange* arrived, she entered her studio to find that the sheep's varnished curls looked cheap. Their pinprick eyes appeared skeptical. Her inspiration board always overflowed with pictures of faces from the golden age of Hollywood. She noticed her pigs were losing weight, more like Jimmy Stewart than Mickey Rooney. Her chickens were more Katherine Hepburn, less Shelley Winters.

Diana understood he had paid a lot for this painted woman-times-three. It was the exact number of his infidelities. She didn't tell him how she found out about Ingrid, the Munich manager. Elsa, Diana saw at Henry's trade convention, and knew at once. She was the organizer, waving red acrylic nails at salesmen desperate to get their quotas up. His ex-wife, he said, didn't really count.

Take it back, she wanted to say. *I don't like it.* Henry would know it was a lie. Then he would think it was a lie when she said she truly forgave him for his mistakes.

With time, Diana noticed, Henry stopped less often in front of the painting. But he sometimes made eye contact with the one looking out before making eye contact with Diana. She began spending long hours in the studio, wearing Henry's old shirts, paint-spattered and hanging limp to her knees. She was determined to have a "body of work." Henry encouraged her, scanned her images into the computer, produced tidy little gift cards. He knew business.

She looked up Costa's work on the Net. She double-clicked on the images, making them large enough for her to view the models close up. In the same way Diana painted the same animals over and over, the artist had used several long-haired women. Diana recognized the one in her kitchen.

Diana selected FAVOURITES, then ADD, and a window came up telling her the site had already been bookmarked. She scrolled down the site to CONTACT and found the artist's email address: tony.costa@rogers.com. Cut and pasted it to add to Henry's address book, but found it was already there.

It seemed right to Diana that they hadn't had sex in a few months. What with Henry's long hours, and the fact that sex naturally waned. Diana accepted his staying late in the city, found herself saying, "If you need to work, I can pack you a dinner." Or "Don't worry, I've got some painting to do tonight." She'd heard the quilters complain about their husbands, having been partnered for decades. They were her elders in the ways of marriage.

"This will put you on the map," he said one evening, handing her the "Bobcaygeon House & Garden Tour" flyer. *View a wonderful selection of traditional and contemporary homes, including several artists' studios, and magnificent gardens. Includes a map and tea and dessert at Trinity United.*

For the two weeks leading up to the tour, he didn't come near the studio. Spent all his spare time weeding and placing tiny wooden signposts in the wildflower beds: CAROLINA SPRING BEAUTY, LADIES' TRESSES, BLACK-EYED SUSAN.

One day Diana began what she thought was a sketch of a huge, rosy apple. It turned into a middle-aged woman studying her body in a full-length mirror, an open book in one hand, her other hand on her hip. The title of the book — *Apple or Pear?* — came quickly, as if Diana had no say. She named the painting *Red Delicious*. Her next piece came quickly too. A grey-haired, wolf-faced lady reading *The Edible Woman* in bed. Next to her lay a sleeping husband, who had a distinctly sheep-like face. And then what she'd intended as a simple sketch of a rabbit turned into drooped ears and dangling legs on a frazzled-looking woman, so that the bunny sat on top of her head. That one she named *One Grey Hare*.

She became curious about all the oversized art books on Henry's shelf. She read about Orlan, an artist who had undergone seven operations to reinvent herself. Plastic surgery had given her the chin of Botticelli's Venus, Mona Lisa's forehead, and the eyes of Diana from a sixteenth-century School of Fontainebleau painting. Art reviewers said her work was a statement about societal pressure to maintain beauty, erase aging. Orlan said no, she was performing the most creative act: her own rebirth. She had chosen women not for their beauty but for their stories. She'd chosen the hunter Diana because of her refusal to give in to gods or men.

Henry had no idea about Diana's new work. She'd heard him speak admiringly of artists' "flow," of their "channelling a greater power." But those were real artists. Some mornings she spent staring out at Henry's wildflowers, the muddle of stems flourishing where they would not naturally grow, and her empty canvas triggered panic. *I'll be found out.* She'd read about the reptilian brain in a first-year psychology class, before she dropped out to try her hand at painting. The primitive centre of the cerebral cortex that humans revert to under threat. She remembered the example the textbook gave of standing outside one's house, searching for one's keys. Then hearing the phone ringing inside.

She began her first papier mâché project the morning she received Tony Costa's reply to her email. She had pretended to be Henry, asking to meet the artist. Costa's prompt and terse reply: I THOUGHT YOU SAID YOU WANTED TO COOL IT FOR A WHILE. The affair didn't surprise her, just the fact that Tony was short for Antonietta. The curves of the woman in the painting suggested the perspective of a heterosexual man. She didn't blame Henry. She'd hidden out with her barnyard animals while Tony sat in triplicate in their kitchen.

For weeks the artist must have donned that dress, set her easel up in front of a full-length mirror, making faces, gesturing, studying herself. Deciding she couldn't be captured in one pose.

And now Diana did the same. She set up a mirror next to the basin of wet paper strips to create the life-size torso. Her fingers pressed the flour paste of the once-lovely face, a nectarine past harvest. She slipped off Henry's shirt, letting it fall back, arms dangling, still tucked into her work pants. She examined her hefty breasts in the oval mirror. Then she sculpted two cow's teats resting on the figure's waist, one veering east, the other west. When the portrait felt dry, she mixed a delicious shade of plum and applied it in blotches simulating cowhide. She lavished the neckline with a creamy peach.

She came in from the studio that night to find Henry sitting at the long table that seemed a continuation of the painting. His arms open wide along the back of the banquette, enjoying the three women's banter.

"I think they're talking about me," he said without looking at Diana. And he held the stare of the model, gave her that grin that used to be reserved solely for Diana.

"I've forgotten something in the studio." Diana rushed back across the path in darkness. Once inside, she didn't turn on the lights. It felt strange, not like a place she'd left moments before. Henry's carefully chosen thermal windows, a theatrical backdrop of black sky and stars. The shadowed trees flat as frames. She remained still until the eyes of the chickens and cows and nascent ladies came into focus. Wet gauze plaster strips hung over the sides of margarine tubs, brushes scattered on the bench. The torso waited on the table with exaggerated nose and lips. She'd never mastered realism.

She would carry her to the house, place her on a high stool next to *The Exchange*. The iron legs would make her appear staunch, determined. "It's called *Udderly Perfect*," she'd say. "Happy belated anniversary."

It won't sell, Henry would say. *It's distasteful.* To bring her art into the house would mess things up, was out of the question. She'd tell him she needed to see her work in a different context, to view it afresh. And then she'd scrub the entire kitchen, right down to a gleaming kettle, pleasing everyone.

DEATH ON THE NILE

We're in line with all the other tour buses leaving Cairo, waiting to join the convoy that travels the highway each morning. Babs, directly in front of me, turns around in her seat. "Do you like being a woman?" she asks.

She's sucking on sugar cane from one of the hawkers who lifted their trays to the bus window. Telling me about the anonymous hands on her ass in Khan el-Khalili, the winding maze of medieval lanes and shops. The boys playing soccer who blocked her way.

"'You are so beautiful,' they said, 'you break my hearts. Will you marry me? Can I call you?' One grabbed my crotch. A man offered his fourteen-year-old son, who proudly escorted me to the main road and a taxi."

Her chin is hooking the top of the seat so it's like the

chair-back is her chest, flat like a boy's. Her fingers gripping the sides.

A young man with a rifle in a cloth bag stands on the step of the bus, talking with Ahmet, the driver. He points to the line of coaches en route to Aswan. "I counted at least twenty-five today," he says. "It's last week's bombing. All Greeks. Damn Islamic militants. Taking it out on the tourists. That's not the way to bring down the government."

I think of the plane ride over, full of pilgrims on their way to Mecca. Wearing only loose white cotton around their loins. Each carrying a tin kettle and cup, their passports in plastic sandwich bags. They didn't know how to use their seat trays. One got out a mat and prostrated in the aisle. They stared at me the whole time. The only Western woman.

I think of my time in Cairo before meeting the "Nile Adventure" group. The absence of women in the streets, a few in full-length burkas. Some attractive women in makeup, hair exposed, driving cars. Not many, though.

Outside the bus, boys balance trays with bottles of pop, passengers play Hacky Sack. I can see men on rooftops of nearby buildings, machine guns beside them like girlfriends.

"I never wanted to be a girl," Babs says.

Now she's talking through the space between the window and her seat. All I see: one brown eye, a gaping nostril, the corner of dry lips. I imagine the puppets she makes in Dublin for movie companies, moving their mouths slowly like she does, matching her thoughts. Try to picture her growing up in Ireland. Chauvinistic men coming on to her, maybe an asshole father believing girls can't be anything more than wives, or a boyfriend pushing her into sex too soon.

I can't see any of it. Babs is frumpy. Her hair is black, the same barbershop cut my mom gave me as a kid. She wears all black, making her pale skin even more anemic. Loose blouses hide her breasts and lack of waist.

"I know what you mean. I was a tomboy too," I say.

"No, I mean I never wanted to be a girl."

I glance at Hal, Babs's husband, doing his daily up-and-down-the-aisle chat, talking to the dozen others on the two-week tour. She says he never wanted to get married. They did it to satisfy his parents. Babs's Cyclops eye scans my face for judgement.

I replay the touchy-feely way Hal and Babs are with each other. It suddenly seems contrived. A normal couple, together ten years, wouldn't behave like that. And Hal has that gay vibe about him: his thick, wavy hair, chunky black glasses, and his immaculate wardrobe, even in the campsites at Giza. He is curt and particular. She is puffy-fingered, always untucked.

The mud houses we pass coming into Aswan are right out of Bethlehem, men in galabiyas on donkeys, straw scattered across stone-walled courtyards. Small scruffy children wave as our convoy passes.

I wonder about women's lives behind stone Nubian walls.

Ahmet is our guide. First meeting, he steps close, his chest in my face, bushy eyebrows looking down at me. "*Habti*, you are beautiful," he says, with the deep belly laugh of an aging Casanova. Except he is younger than me, probably no more than nineteen, in Western jeans and an Armani T-shirt. When he smiles, I notice his chin takes up half his face. His tag line: "Any questions? C'mon, I love questions. Any questions from the ladies?"

He drives us to the wooden feluccas I've seen only in pictures, angular sails like white pen nibs. His bus sweeps through streets of vans, pedestrians, donkey carts. He's worked it so the first two rows are full of women. Egyptian music cranked, he's moving Nubian style, both hands off the wheel, flicking his chunky fingers at the windscreen, horn tooting in time to the music. He turns around on the last two beats of each phrase and taps his face twice towards me, as if trying to detach his head from his neck.

Ahmet stops at Qahwa Café. The group stretches their legs, orders tea in small glasses. I watch him play backgammon with Samir, another driver. The show is for me. The slap-slam of markers, the argument with hands and guttural sounds ending in smiles. Ahmet leans over and makes faces. Orders me thick, sweet Egyptian coffee. Then he passes me the shisha. I suck in and watch the water bubble through the glass. It's strong and I'm buzzed.

He changes the mouthpiece, sucks on it slowly, looking at me. "Remind you of anything?"

I don't smile.

"*Habti*, in your eyes I see you are sad, like you are thinking of someone in the past. Back home."

"Look, Ahmet, every tour the guide picks someone. It's like it's written in the fine print. *Start day one. You've got a week to close the deal.*" I do two Nubian head taps.

"You are a disaster," he says with a smile, just like the gem sellers when they begin to barter.

Three days on the Nile. Two feluccas. Single boat, married boat. Seven of us lie on one big tarp staring up at the huge sail with a rip in it. Playing cards, reading, sleeping. The silence of white fabric tacking towards Luxor, my body changing angles on the keel. Two men cook dinner in the cramped hull. They lay out a square mat above deck for chicken, rice, and vegetables. They smoke reefer non-stop and sleep on our bags in the bow.

On the first night the stoned crew paddles all night, everyone snoring. This guy named Warren and I are the only two awake. He kills me with a wink. We're playing Death on the Nile. The murderer has to kill everyone before he's found out, before we reach Luxor.

"Did you get it?" he whispers. I nod. But I don't die. I want to save my death, die dramatically.

Warren has a GI-on-a-day-pass look, uncomfortable in the real world, hair refusing to grow beyond a buzz cut. He's eight years my junior. His needle nose and serious eyes pull me in, but only because I'm lonely. The inaccessible world of marriage is up close on this trip. Craig, the cop, and his figure-skating wife, Jinny. Two retired professors who've sold their home to travel. Even Hal and Babs have worked out a sympatico partnership.

Our sleeping bags are open, our hands wandering. Someone sits up in the dark, a mummy wrapped in blankets, then lies back down.

"I think someone's watching, Warren."

"I don't give a goddamn."

We whisper and stifle giggles as if our parents are upstairs.

"I need to pee," I say. "Where's the ramp?"

I'm standing on the bow, laughing. The crew have forgotten to put the beam out over the water. I hold on to a rope, squat, and lean out as far as I can as the boat pitches.

Warren kisses badly. It's as if the pressure in his pants

has gone to his lips, and it hurts my mouth. In my mind I climb to the tip of the mast, watching us. It's always like this. Waiting for the moves to be executed. Hoping the slobbering mouth gives up or the beard doesn't leave too much burn. A little breast-fumbling, a little rubbing, sliding hands. I focus on the lunar eclipse, a perfect, shining ring.

"We are sailing down the Nile," I say.

"We're going at quite a pace," he says. "I'm not talking about the boat."

"All we did was kiss, Warren."

"So what happens now?"

"We go to sleep," I say.

We dock the boats at Kom Ombo Temple. There are carvings everywhere of penises dripping with sperm, births, scenes of suckling. Osiris, father of Horus, was cut up into a million pieces, and Isis searched the world, gathering parts, but couldn't find his penis. He couldn't be returned to human status without it.

"That's all it takes to be a man, eh?" Babs says. We stare at Horus's falcon head, human body.

"I heard there was some action on your felucca. Poor Warren, he's smitten. Ahmet would be seriously jealous if he found out. So many men around you, eh?"

"Why, though?"

"Because you smile."

"That's it?"

"You're so open."

"I guess I don't smile at home."

"We're all different on vacation."

"Are you?"

"I'm learning to be. From you."

"In Canada I work from home, plugging numbers into spreadsheets. I get takeout in the same Chinese restaurant every night. Dish 117 on Mondays and Wednesdays and dish 63 on Tuesdays and Thursdays. On Fridays I walk an extra block for a slice of pizza. No one along the way tells me I'm beautiful."

Farther up the Nile, at the Daraw Camel Market, Mohammed the camel seller asks me to leave the convoy, become his wife, tells me I'm worth four thousand camels. He shows me his passport, a photo of a handsome young boy in 1925. It's my first marriage proposal of the day. The second is from a policeman in a purple sweater sitting on the stone wall where we dock the feluccas, machine gun strapped to his chest.

It's too windy to sail, so we're moored most of the afternoon. The Canadians on the boat talk about the Hale-Bopp cult deaths in Quebec. The news says they packed their suitcases and dressed in black shirts, black pants, and running shoes. Then, over several days, they ate barbiturate-laced pudding and applesauce and drank vodka chasers. One by one they lay down, holding their ID, believing they would be airlifted by a heaven-bound UFO.

"We should die together," Babs says. She's already guessed Warren is It. "Let's make it an event."

A young boy appears on the sand with his baby sister. So blond and blue-eyed I forget I'm in Egypt. A man named Farach Farat comes to the shore, invites everyone to his house nearby. He farms mangos, bananas, cows, sheep. It's a Nubian house made of mud and bricks, dirt floor. A stone oven in the corridor. The inner sanctuary holds thick butter from the cow. There is one room with a big bed.

He holds up six dirty fingers, the number in his family. Farach tours us through his property. His wife stands in a doorway in a long, dusty dress, head covered, holding her baby. Her eyes flat and dark, looking at our bare legs and independence. The grandmother in black, enjoying our invasion, the cameras.

The living room consists of two mats and a black-and-white TV. We sit cross-legged with Farach and the kids, eating bread, sweet cakes, tea. Watch an Egyptian soap opera with heavily mascaraed women tilting their heads in sorrow. Four pages from German fashion magazines are stuck to the blue walls with Scotch tape.

Next door to the house, a stable of twelve cows. We give Farach baksheesh, which he folds into his wallet, and later he carries a bleating lamb down to the boat, offering to slaughter it for our dinner. The women on our boats shake their heads, wave their hands no. He comes back to our campfire with a drum and a miniature white horse, to show how it lifts its legs on the beats.

Warren hovers on the felucca, waiting to see where I'm going to lay out my sleeping bag. I spread my mat out with my back to him.

"What happened?" he asks. "Did I do something wrong?"

"It was cold that night, Warren."

"I can't believe this," he says.

When Ahmet finds out about Warren, I see him moving in on Karen from South Africa. He tells her he thinks she's sad, holding on to something from her past, as he stares at her breasts. Ahmet says he chose her from the beginning and will she live in Egypt? "Sit with us," I tell her.

Ahmet is sulking. In the middle of the night I hear, "Karen, have you made your decision yet?"

Babs is lightest when we are in the market, bartering for stones, lapis lazuli, turquoise. She's come to rely on me for the best deal. The merchant starts at twenty-five Egyptian pounds for one gold ring. I get three for fifty. I don't know this version of me: smiling when he starts high; hand on my hip, starting low; heading for the door when he says he won't go lower; then hearing "We are so close, *madame*. Can we not meet halfway?" If he says "fixed price," I laugh like a man, say, "C'mon, let's have some fun."

"How do you do that?" Babs asks.

"You just have to decide before you start: how much am I willing to pay? As long as you know where you stand."

Ahmet gets two hotel suites at Edfu, for everyone to wash. Before we head into the room, Hal says, "Are all you women showering together?"

"It only matters if you're both sexes," Babs says.

"What?" I say.

She stares at Jinny in her white undies a moment longer than a straight woman would. I hit her and laugh. It occurs to me that Babs meant herself, that she is both male and female. Jinny goes all quiet, then disappears into the bathroom.

"God, I'm a bull in a china shop," Babs says.

She and I are the only two who go swimming before dinner. We slip into the shallow end, the rest of the group either in the café at the far end or snoozing on benches.

Babs's bathing suit is black, her body puffy like dough.

Her tummy protrudes farther than her chest. Her skin is translucent, like the jellyfish I saw when I snorkelled in the Red Sea. My bathing suit is the colour of their purple centres. We float like shisha bubbles. There's nowhere to go, no hawker to fight with, no merchant to cover up from, no machine guns protecting us here. The barbed-wire fence, the walls around the pool, a reprieve from campsites. Babs floats on her back, her breasts half out the sides of her halter top. Nipples caught by the zigzag stitching so they're covered: tiny, perfect gems.

She spreads out her arms and legs like a kid lying in snow. In Hurghada she wouldn't go in the sea, said she wasn't a confident swimmer, so I know this act is pure abandonment. She stays very still. Her white bathing cap is like a lure. I watch the water surround her face, leaving a mask of eyes, nose, and mouth, without wrinkles, without age. She is a newborn the moment before a harsh entrance. I breaststroke over to her, careful not to disturb.

I dive down and speak underwater. "Babs." So she will hear my sound and won't startle at my touch.

I run my hands down the backs of her thighs and calves, then up again to the place where her suit meets skin. Feel the coarse hair lying flat against her mound. Then my hands travel up her back, her uneven spine, as if tracing the Nile, the most fertile river in the world, our path through Egypt. I stay underwater and swim to the ledge. Look up to see if anyone's watching. They're lost in books, writing journals, pouring beer.

I push my feet off from the wall, towards Babs. She's still floating, eyes closed. I circle her this time, place my hand in the curve of her back as if holding her up. I notice the undersides of her arms, which are usually covered. They are full of cuts, from elbow to wrist, some fresh, some healed over. Red and pink. None of them straight; none of them have done the job. I paddle away, hover near the ledge, watching her the way we scan the dusty horizon when Ahmet calls "mirage" from the front of the bus.

On safari with the Bedouins, Babs and I are able to ride side by side when Skyhan, my camel, cooperates. A seven-year-old boy on foot smacks him, yells *"Hareea!"* The camel bolts and the boy runs, herding him back into line. Babs and I sit on mattresses tied on top of the saddles, the ones we will sleep on tonight under Orion's belt and the Big Dipper. We talk about Egyptian men.

"What about that egomaniac Ramses II? The temple of Abu Simbel is a work of genius — four hundred feet high, a hundred thousand tons — but it's all just so the light can shine into that inner sanctum twice a year, on him and his sun-god pals."

"You missed the army guy in Suez, Babs. He rode his motorcycle right into this kid on a bicycle, wrecked his back wheel. He just took off. A few minutes later, a bunch of his army buddies pulled up and jumped on the wheel to straighten it out. The kid got on his bicycle and rode away."

"Those are the kind of men you want drinking killer Kool-Aid. Hale-Bopp to them."

"No H words, Babs!" Skyhan's itching to break away.

At night we put all our mattresses together as if we're a felucca in the desert. We eat a dinner of rice and potatoes, play some cards, choose our bedmates. Ahmet's head on my stomach, face too close to my breasts. He hands me binoculars to look at the Hale-Bopp comet, but it's a disappointing shooting star. The Bedouins stay up late by the campfire burning palm leaves, their eyes glowing, a loud boom box with disco lights. "They are waiting for dirty dancing," Ahmet says. None of us go close to the fire. I ask if there are snakes here, spend a sleepless night watching two shapes that seem to move and get closer. In the morning I see I have been staring at rocks.

The bulk of blankets beside each camel is a Bedouin. They slowly wake, walk their animals, feed them acacia leaves. The order of loading: pretty blond women first. They warn us to keep the camel's heads out of each other's asses; it's shagging time. Hal climbs on his camel and we watch it saunter over and attempt to mount Babs's camel. Hal bends forward, holding on to the neck, screaming "*Yella!*" It continues to rock like a coin-operated grocery-store horse until the trainers yank its rope.

King Tut's tomb is a disappointment. We walk through empty corridors that twist and turn, down wooden staircases to the enormous stone room where his coffin lies empty. Babs, Warren, and I are way ahead of the rest of the gang.

"C'mon," she says, her voice bouncing off the high ceiling. Babs lies down in the coffin on her back. It's a perfect fit. She places her hands over her chest and closes her eyes, like the mummies in the Cairo Museum. She says, "Hale-Bopp, Hale-Bopp, Hale-Bopp." Stays dead for a while. Warren avoids eye contact with me.

She finally climbs out and I go next. Then Warren takes a turn, following my every move. He points up at the video camera and we meander back, wondering if we're going to get arrested at the exit. But the guards are too busy snoozing.

On the final day of our tour, the boats anchor at Luxor. I hear Warren whisper to Ahmet, "Why won't anyone die? I killed them all."

Babs takes my hand and presses a piece of turquoise into it. The one shaped like the fertile valley, already drilled with a hole for a necklace. The one she desperately wanted, asked me to barter for in Aswan. She kisses me on the lips, mouth closed, holding there as if sealing an important document.

There are a few last-minute deaths. Someone keels over on deck, and "Killing Me Softly" comes over the loudspeaker. It's Craig, who's spent the whole trip in a Bedouin galabiya because he says it lets things breathe better down there. He stumbles on the sand.

"If the guys at the precinct get a picture of me in this dress, I'm dead." He takes out a knife and gives himself a full-on Julius Caesar stabbing.

Babs suddenly stands up. We are both wearing black, holding our backpacks and white plastic cups. I grab her hand and step to the bow of our felucca. The marrieds on their felucca watching. We join hands, sit cross-legged, chant "Hale-Bopp," and point up at an imaginary comet. Pretending something so far from home can influence who we are. We take a swig from our cups, then, holding our ID to our chests, we fall back dead. My passport shoots out of my hand but I catch it just before it disappears into the Nile.

UP UP UP

His left top lip twitches when he makes love, as if pulled by a marionette's string. Saying *up up up*.

"You're so big," I say. I know that keeps him there. Eyes looking down on me like in a fantasy. So I push my luck, say, "Let's make a baby." I know he's far away. *Let's make a baby* — the words attached to my insides. I have him now. He'll give that to me in the next few minutes. His eyes flick, dark like his brain has fallen in, asking, *Should I be thinking about this?* And then he remembers. All those years of smoking. All those years of unprotected sex. *Baby* goes back to being an empty word like *big* or *suck* or *harder*. It spurs him on, knowing there's nothing but nothingness to give.

My legs high in the air, willing it to go as far as it can

go. Picturing the rubbing of my belly, the soft smiles on our faces as we walk the neighbourhood, dreaming of dresses and soccer balls and pushes on swings.

I grab my ankles, *up up up*, fall into the word *baby*. Let my insides tumble out. His lip twitches a while after.

‹ ‹ ‹

My twenty little kindergarteners are on the red and blue climber. Snaking and laddering as they call, "Miss D! Look at me! Look, Miss D." As they take the biggest risks of their lives.

Elsie is off on her own. Short boy-hair in her fairy dress. She's the youngest in the class. Born premature, with a weakened ventricle in her heart. "If she ever turns blue, call 911," her mother says.

In class Elsie often tires of me. All my counting and clapping patterns and giving instructions. The others sit cross-legged, spellbound by this thing called school, this thing they've been dreaming of since their older siblings began going every day. Elsie often decides she's had enough and gets up off the carpet, wanders over to Cut and Paste or the Kitchen Centre, to put the dolls in a carriage. She takes them for a spin around the room. When I call to her, she sighs and sits on the carpet with her back to me, studies her feet, lies down, undies exposed, until one of the senior kindergarteners scolds her.

Today Elsie is off skipping by herself on the playground while the others fight for a turn on the slide. I watch her trip on her dress and, *boom*, she's down. I wait for the cry and the run to me. I wait for sound. Instead she gets up and

walks farther away, to the sandbox. Sits on the edge, hugs
her knees. Mouth open as if it's stuck.

I run to her. Under her right eye is a bloody cut. Her knee
a patch of grated skin. I leave my assistant with the others,
collect her like a load of laundry from the dryer, run into
the school. Set her down near the sink in the classroom.
Crouching so I'm looking up at her.

"It'll be gone soon. It'll be all right. It'll be gone." I
realize she's been chanting this since I picked her up in the
yard. It's as if she's in the room alone. I'm wiping the bloody
scrape an inch from her eye. Her eyelashes clumped like star-
points. She's looking up at the windows of the classroom.
The changing maples we've been tracking throughout the
year, from gold and red to stark black to bud. All that green
now. I have not stopped to turn on the lights. So the sun
through the trees lands on her face in a tremble. I can feel
she's filling herself, the way the yard inevitably comes alive
in spring. And I'm there dabbing with a wet paper towel,
wishing I had Polysporin, something soft.

"There," I say. The Band-Aid is on.

"It's all better now. All better," she's chanting. It's
calming me. "My knee's all better." Her eyes are small and
she's heading for the door, the playground. Where she runs
ahead. The hem of her dress and her arms out like a bell,
little feet running.

I blow the whistle for all to line up. Elsie at the back.
Always the last to hear the signal.

"Are you okay, Elsie? What happened to Elsie?" the
children near her ask. They're looking at her face.

"She fell. She was so brave," I tell them.

"No, she wasn't. She was crying," another little girl says.

I take a step towards the front of the line. The parents are waiting to pick their children up. We're late. I turn back.

"To cry is the bravest thing of all," I say. It's one of those rare moments when their little bodies have stopped. My words go in like the last piece of a long worked-out puzzle. We head in. Elsie's mother is at the door.

"What happened?" she asks in a high pitch that triggers Elsie's tears. She collapses in her mother's arms. My body perfectly still now. Watching the baby in Elsie coming out now. Watching her give that to her mom.

‹ ‹ ‹

Put the headphones on. Lie belly-down on the bed. Sunday afternoon. Shades half down. Half light. Jane Siberry singing, *Come on, come on, come on*. I put my hand down the front of my jeans. Lie on my arm as if it's you. Like it's you feeling the weight. She's singing loud now. Music like layers of covers I'm under and the clouds are moving over the walls, the light changing every time my fingers move. My eyes close. Chin pressing like a pea into the mattress. I picture you coming into the room. Your hand on my lower back. *Let me finish you off*, you say. Your hand asking me to step off the cliff. Asking me to push, like labour. To push you out, fuck you out. *It's better than crying*, your hand says. And the music and the clouds are all rooting for me. Pulsing like a Greek dance sped up at a wedding. The sweaty groom afraid of his feet, the bride glowing, not in thought anymore, just moving in the swirl of white lace, in a story she only dreamt of.

SPECULATORS

THE PIT

That summer we learn about rape. A Girl Guide from our unit goes into the valley one late afternoon and comes out different. During Opening Circle we stare at her face, looking for what it is. She wears her shiny hair in a ponytail now, pulled straight back. Not high up the way my Nan does my hair.

Nan wants to be a beautician. Whenever Mom leaves her to babysit, I end up with a Shirley Temple perm and eyelids the colour of our blue toilet.

"She looks like a tart," my mom says. The only tarts I know are the kind I pick raisins out of or the Queen of Hearts, who lost hers. I don't agree with my mother but I am not part of the conversation. I lie low so Nan will be allowed to babysit again.

Girls aren't to go into the valley, though. Not by ourselves. A man is in the valley. "But it was daylight. She was with her little sister," we hear the adults say, as if disputing the softball schedule. "Why did Alison's parents let them walk home that way? Wasn't she trained not to talk to strangers?" They need someone to blame.

I understand, after the talk settles, that at the bottom of it is the girl. She made it happen. She walked down into it with part of her, as small as a Girl Guide pin, knowing.

In junior high it's called the Pit. We know it's somewhere in the valley near York Mills and Don Mills. Boys smoke up and drink. Sunday afternoons, Cindy Stokes and I lie in Sharon Trane's basement listening to AC/DC: *Dirty deeds and they're done dirt cheap / She's got the biggest balls of them all.* Put on our stoner jackets, woodcutter plaid, and pile into Sharon's parents' orange Chevette, determined to find the Pit in daylight so we can return at night. Windows down, cigarettes hanging from our fingertips like we're film noir vixens. Sharon with her Farrah Fawcett bangs and Cindy with her polka-dot nail stickers. The road winds near York Mills and Sharon drives fast, sticking her arm straight out to match mine on the other side, flapping: *we're flying.* That makes us giggle no matter what.

We've surveyed the area for a year, deciding on the clump of trees closest to an empty parking lot. We walk single file on the pencil trail, farther and farther, until daylight turns dark green and we stand totally lost in the forest. Part of us doesn't believe in the Pit, until we see that tiny orange ribbon nailed to a tree. The roots cleave to a ten-foot drop, a bowl of dry earth, burnt logs. Just like the middens in our geography textbook but with empty Coors Light bottles. It looks harmless, welcoming.

We come out on the other side of the field, have to walk a long way around to Sharon's Chevette but it doesn't matter. We've found the Pit.

This calls for McDonald's, a celebratory sundae. We scan the cars at each stoplight for boys checking us out.

"Hey, don't look behind. That's a cop following us," Sharon says into the rear-view mirror.

They probably think we're high-on-something Pit girls and we are so not. Sharon's running low on gas, driving anywhere but home, hands on ten and two the way they taught in driving school. The cops give up after about five miles.

Next Friday night we return, irresistible cats with roll-on cherry lips and liquid-liner eyes. Our feet remembering the trail in the dark. Voices help us find the orange marker. We peer down at a small fire, boys perched on logs, cigarettes held to their mouths in a way we know it isn't tobacco. We walk around the perimeter, quiet, not cracking any twigs or anything, hidden, safe. *We'll have enough courage soon.*

"Hey, girls." We freeze like it's tag, the last game of our lives.

"Hey, girls, why doncha come down?" Deep boy laughter, clink of beer bottles. My heartbeat so loud I stop breathing, not giving it oxygen to continue. But that makes it go faster, and I can hear Cindy's and Sharon's heartbeats too. One big knocking so we'll wake up and run. It's like we're deciding whether to stay, to descend into the Pit. To be a tart. The boys hoping we'll figure it out.

CUPBOARDS OPEN

"What'd you end up doing last night?"

"I lay on my bedroom floor and cried for two hours. Then I phoned all my friends to make sure they still love me."

"That's one way to spend an evening," I say.

Sue stares at me as if she's deciding to give me my Christmas present early. "You know," she says, "I've never seen you raw. Or madly in love. I've never seen you really angry or really sad or really anything. It's like you feel the feeling and then contain it with humour. Or by saying *Okay, I'm strong.*"

"Oh."

"And if someone else is sad, you feel it, then you scoop it up and say, *I'll be strong for both of us.* Even your body is contained."

I don't ask what that means. She looks innocent enough with all those freckles. I wait. Maybe I'm containing the moment.

"Are you happy with that? I mean, if you're comfortable with that, that's great. Do you have a way of releasing it? I want that for you."

I know what Sue wants. Confession. We've come to Sunnybrook Park for a picnic lunch on a break from vocal class. The ducks surround our table, squawking for scraps. I've forgotten a spoon for my salad and I make one out of a pipe cleaner I have in my purse. The white fuzzy bits mix in with the couscous and I like the effect. Sue seems annoyed at that.

I finish telling her my theory of detour. How I'm right where I want to be, then someone or something takes me off track. A job, a man. A year, five years — every time I arrive back at the place I've given up. I look out over the river, which is a good thing to do when you're describing dramatic arcs in life. The sparkling eddies and trees encouraging me with swooshing noises.

"Look at me. Eyes on me." Sue says this twice as I'm talking. I bring my eyes back to her. Maybe she's mimicking our music teacher. Maybe liars don't make eye contact. Maybe she's sensing that I'm not being raw. I contain my eye contact.

"I don't get sideswiped by men," Sue says. "I'm exploring unrequited love. I know Stan doesn't love me. I've had people so in love with me, lots of people, and I never returned it and it's all okay. When I'm in love, I just have so much more to give the world. Love is love."

One of the ducks pecks at my toe as if it's a french fry.

"Hey! I have nothing for you!" I say.

When I visit my parents that night, they are arguing at the dinner table. My mother is pleased to see me.

"Your father has so many idiosyncrasies. He cuts the tops off the cereal boxes as the flakes go down. And he fills his teacup till it can't hold another drop, then drinks only half. And the cupboards. I spend half my life going around closing the kitchen cupboards. Why can't he close them?"

"And you have no idiosyncrasies?" he says. "I don't do

it on purpose."

"I do have idiosyncrasies, but if you know it bothers me — and he knows it bothers me because I've told him — if you still do it, then that's on purpose, right?" She turns to me, expecting me to be crazy enough to step into this.

"I don't leave the doors open on purpose."

"I swear, if he keeps doing it I'll leave him. It's honestly enough to make me leave."

I think of all the people in love, dying to get into this married world. Before I go to bed, I leave the cupboard below the sink open, and the one by the fridge.

KNOWING PERFECTLY

Ruth's saleslady-on-commission face greets me at the door.

"What happened? You get lost? Didn't you go north on Yonge?"

"Yeah, but they moved the municipal building. It's a Tim Hortons now."

We giggle nervously at that. At what's coming.

I can see Ruth's husband, Norm, with the smile that always seems bigger because of the two chins. He's gesturing to you but I can't see you yet in the living room, making small talk, timing it perfectly for when I round the corner. I take off my shoes because Ruth's mahogany hall table and plush carpet tell me to. Little grooved waves there in the weave, like water I'm about to fall into. I think of this to prolong the moment.

Norm looks up in the space in conversation and Ruth parts the air so I can make a proper entrance.

"This is Paul! Ray's uncle!" Ruth's voice from behind me, the same back-of-the-house timbre she used to convince me in the first place. *So handsome, so fit.*

I see your grin, trying for irony, like this whole thing is just our little joke. You sit with your legs open like a turkey wishbone, feet tight together at the snapping part. Your round belly in the crux. Knee-high socks pulled up tight. Beige shorts, beige shirt, puffy face. And when you stand, I see you're tiny, like the jars of jam I used to get in my Christmas stocking that covered only half my toast.

Think, *Who's the leprachaun?*

Say, "Finally."

The moment you stand, I see two china plates, Charles and Di on their wedding day, like round antlers above your head. So many witnesses.

I smile right into you, looking for the face of Ray, the boy I used to watch at the local theatre, the star who swept his broom across the stage with the presence of Arlequino, knowing perfectly when to linger, when to leave. Who surprised the hell out of me in the final scene as a suitor at the foot of his lover's balcony, drooping roses, red plaid suit, singing operatic gibberish in falsetto.

Your beige fishing hat, ears like pincushions. *He swims every day and he owns a sailboat!* I see the kid far back in those tiny blue eyes, under lids of skin, English garden eyebrows. It's an Academy Award for me holding your gaze. Not even a shade pulls down. I mirror your grin.

You take off your hat, your hair a thick Berber carpet, Clairol Nice 'n Easy brown. Then your arms are out, but instead of a hug you swing me around and hook me into the armpit so we're facing Ruth and Norm. Your too-tight hand clutching my arm as if we're about to make an important announcement. Ruth saying, "I've a good feeling about this."

I see the whole life of the living room, the window balloon dressing, the striped wallpaper, the pillows, probably yellows and browns and beiges. I don't name the colours right at this moment but I know they all match, with accents picked up here, referenced there. I know there's a plan that's revealed itself over the years. The clusters of knick-knacks, the photographs of children, stepchildren, grandchildren, pets.

And later, after you let me choose which Johnny Cash tape to listen to on the way to the Sportsmen's Show, after you tell me Stuart McLean anecdotes and touch my arm to punctuate certain points, after you say *shit* and *fuck* like any cool guy would and *neat* when I catch the one tagged metal disc in the casting pond and receive my glow-in-the-dark Crappie Killer jig ("You will improve your hook-up ratio"), after you lend me your jacket so I can stand really close to the dock at the Big Air Dog Jump and you lift your hand to show me your baby finger stitches where your beagle almost chewed right through, and after you say you hadn't been sure you'd make the date but were determined, and I stick out my fingernail half gone from my new puppy and it's the very same pinkie, after you let it slip that you've got my number on speed dial, after you start so many sentences, then say my name halfway through so that I know you're there with me completely, that I've slipped into something that's been waiting — after all that we stand in the driveway as you search the back seat for your other fishing hat. Norm and Ruth wait with their arms around each other's waists and I'm watching you put on your windbreaker, adjust the blue cap on your head. I see you using these props, drawing out the moment before you ask me out again. Before you decide on the words under the gaze of our matchmakers. Those who have gone before us. I stand there. Waiting for the scene. Like a dumb new actor. Doubting the career choice. Doubting the ending will surprise me.

ACKNOWLEDGEMENTS

Versions of some of these stories have previously appeared in literary publications: "Up Up Up" and "Encounter" in *Particle & Wave: An Anthology of New Fiction* (Mansfield Press, 2007); "Levitate" and "Speculators" in *The New Quarterly*; "The Tree Man" and "Geology in Motion" in *PRISM International*; "Every Good Boy" in *Exile*; and "How Fast Things Go" in *Prairie Fire* and *Best Canadian Stories* (Oberon Press, 2010). Many thanks to the editors of these publications. I am also grateful to the Ontario Arts Council for its support over the years.

Thanks to Melanie Little for her editorial acumen; Sarah MacLachlan and the good folks at Anansi for being so enthusiastic; Alissa York for her wise guidance and the Banff Wired Writing Studio for bringing us together; Lisa

Moore for her example and advice; Janet Bailey, whose paintings inspired "The Exchange"; my parents for a lifetime of loving support and auto maintenance; my Nan for her geraniums; Eleanor Wachtel for the imaginary interview I've been rehearsing for twenty years; and Denis for trading a golden retriever for a toy poodle without blinking an eye.